Perspectives of You and Me

Liona McMahon

© 2017 Liona McMahon
Herstellung und Verlag: BoD – Books on Demand, Norderstedt.

ISBN: 9783743182387

This is a work of fiction. Names, characters, businesses, places, events and incidents are either the products of the author's imagination or used in a fictitious manner. Any resemblance to actual persons, living or dead, or actual events is purely coincidental.

Content

Lynne   2015   *Lynne   2016*

Lynne   1998   *Al   2016*

Lynne   2015   *Lynne   2016*

Al   1998   *Ben   2016*

Lynne   1998   *Lynne   2016*

Ben   2015   *Ben   2016*

Lynne   2015   *Lynne   1998*

Lynne   1998   *Lynne   1999*

Lynne   2015   *Lynne   2016*

Cam   2015   *Ben   2016*

Lynne   2015   *Cam   2016*

Lynne   1998

Lynne   2016

Lynne, 2015

Lost in thoughts. So deep one doesn't really know what kind. Like one's body is just drifting somewhere in nowhere, and yet heavy as a rock, with a feeling that is probably best described as numbness. All physical senses dampened, soggy...numb. Like you feel the moment after getting slapped good and hard in the face, after assuming an argument was of verbal nature.

I experienced this feeling every single morning the minute I was ruggedly torn from sleep - when this seldom state ever occurred - stumbled out of bed, dizzy with low blood pressure, and into the kitchen to make a satisfyingly filling breakfast consisting of coffee, a cig and - if there was time - a slice of toast.

And it continued when I left the house, second fag in one hand, handbag - if it was remembered - in the other. And when I reached the small, "quaint" entrance of the photo studio and shop I worked in and managed with the help of one assistant. Once there, some thoughts could be blocked, my senses restored to a point that allowed me to work with my hands and eyes effectively.

After all, to do one's work professionally includes some blocking out of thoughts and to concentrate on what the senses were doing. *My* work did, anyway.

I was a photographer. How great it had been to have found someone willing to take on a socially awkward, rather uncommunicative teenager, to work my way up to be a very good photographer and to finally find a small place with a "for sale" sign near where Al and I had lived.

And what a battle it had been against that ex of mine, my ex-boss and the cash seemingly seeping from my purse when I looked away to finally climb to the top of the ladder of self employment. I had been hoping for just that since I had started my training at the age of seventeen.

Now, more than fifteen years later, I was clutching desperately to a step just below with one hand after the top one had snapped.

This September morning was one of those days...

For god's sake, it's six? I just got into effing bed. And that bloody dream... Not one minute of decent sleep. Again. There's the dizziness, I'm going to have to get that checked.

Doesn't diabetes make you dizzy? I could be pregnant, haha.

Those were the superficial, rather cynical thoughts that usually went through my head on an ordinary morning. Down beneath, whirling about like leaves in a bad storm, were more sincere, dismal ones the numbness seemed to keep from coming to the surface.

What would happen if I were forced to close the shop? How long 'til I had to seriously think about filing for impending insolvency? I hadn't wanted Al's money or Cam's…

Expenses for just basic needs like food, clothes and accommodation were already held at a minimum. I ought to look for a smaller place - not only because the previous flat was overflowing with memories. I no longer got bottled water and had lost 3 pounds saving on food (or whatever new metric system one used to determine the weight of something these days, I'd lost a few inches anyways.)

What's it going to be for tea later on?

What else could I do to get my finances running smoothly? Was I going to get customers in?

That mum's coming in with her son to get his passport photos...Was that today?

Had they stopped coming because of the state the place was in? Or was it me that they weren't all that keen on?

Door's looking a bit come down...

Perhaps it was because we'd arrived in the age of the smartphone and a perfectly good family-photo could be taken with a selfie-stick. Much cheaper and less time consuming than a professional photo-shooting, I supposed...

It had all been easier when Al had been there to support me. Where was he? What was he thinking? Had he found someone?

Idiot couldn't even get that fixed before he pissed off.

Al.

How I missed his laugh when watching his favorite sitcoms and the way he made cheese sauce. I never got cheese sauce right. It always went lumpy.

Why was I incapable of keeping anything that was important to me in life?

Cam was just about all I had left. Would my way of expressing myself chase her away eventually too?

Better not miss coffee with Cam at 1 after standing her up yesterday.

"… here to get Stanley's photos. Are they ready? If we're too early we can come back in the afternoon…" With her bustling about, trying to get some dust off the shelves, I hadn't heard the customers enter the studio.

Where's Miles? This is what he was planning on doing. It this his day off? Again?

It was near a main road, so the noise of cars driving past with 70 miles per hour where 47 were allowed was probably a good enough excuse.

"I...sorry? Oh. Stanley ... Brighton? Here we are."

I handed them over to the ginger woman who showed them to her son, a rather heavy looking boy with rather bad skin, aged about 13. He looked at the photos, then eyed me in a way that was probably supposed to be dismissive, as he had when they'd been there the first time. I wasn't sure, as the excess fat in his face seemed to limit the motor ability in that area and thus the ability to express emotions.

Maybe there aren't any.

"That doesn't look like me."

His tone matched the expression that had, I discovered once more, been very dismissive indeed.

"Now, Stan, don't be like that. You want to look nice when people look at your passport. We're going on a nice holiday soon, remember?"

I found it fascinating that this kind of mum-son relationship actually existed outside bad comedies.

"You don't think I look just fine?"

"Nonsense, Stanny, you're just perfect."

Too much airbrushing, apparently.

I had seen to most of the spots and attempted to make the hair seem a tad less greasy.

I hadn't been sure if the boy had been sweating on the hot August afternoon or if his hair had been dripping…

"Fine. Good bye." He said - or rather spat – as they turned to leave. His mother gave me the money for the photos, muttered "I'm so sorry for his behavior. Puberty, it's been going on for weeks…" and went after him. "If they don't recognize me and don't let me into the stupid plane, it's your-" I heard him shout just before the door fell shut.

I finally exhaled. A bit of good will could have cost me another customer.

Why was I being so hard on myself? No one'd EVER complained. That kid was simply a wee shite.

Maybe I should start asking people if they even want photos edited.

Was I maybe not fit for the job if I wasn't capable of seeing natural beauty?

But, I reminded myself, of course I could bloody well see it. The reason I wanted to, always *had* wanted to take pictures, was just that. To capture flowers, animals, moments like the kiss of a bride and groom, a baby's first smile, the silly face on someone blowing out candles on a birthday cake. And other sappy, emotional stuff.

It had just been in the last four years or so my work had been limited to passport photos and the occasional family or baby portrait. The reason my diet had been limited to coffee, toast and noodles with tomato ketchup.

Might be time to get off these, another packet emptied...might help save a few quid a month.

Lynne, 1998

Life's complicated. The sheer existence of it is so complex that humanity has until today failed to understand exactly how it all works, how are we supposed to understand small details of it such as emotions, senses, moods, instincts... That might be why it lies in our nature to act irrational at times. Fight, start wars, hurt others, take drugs... Because we don't understand. We don't get it. And probably never will or won't for a long, long time. But if we knew how to act properly every second of every day, would we even be human? Would love, kindness, happiness and all of those things be real and genuine if that were all there was to feel?

Similar thoughts go through the minds of most adults at some point in their life, when they have moments to themselves with nothing specific to do. When sitting in the train on their way to work, when waiting for the kettle to finish boiling.

Children, on the other hand, worry about not wanting to go to school but having to anyway, getting scolded by parents and teachers for being wee shits - sorry, misbehaving -, about what they want for Christmas but might not get.

They cry because another child runs into them accidently, causing them to fall, or because they want a toy they don't get the very moment they demanded it. Not - or, rather, rarely - with joy or relief because a football match is won, or because the baby of a beloved friend is born.

The kid that had fallen off the swing beside me (not from a great height, more like stumbled in the attempt to elegantly descend) and was currently being seen to by a teacher, was crying in a particularly and increasingly high volume. Why?

I didn't understand kids. Even though I'd been one just a few years back.

And I understood adults even less. Even though I was merely a couple of years away from being (regarded as) one (legally).

My thoughts didn't often go that deep.

The only things I thought about very much currently were getting through school without putting too much effort into learning, spending time with myself and a good book or, more importantly, alone with Greg's camera and some images worth capturing.

Basically, that was all I wanted to do since the day I'd been permitted to use Greg's camera, the love of his life or rather second love of his life, considering the passion that lay in his gaze when he looked at his wife Phoebe.

Greg and Phoebe were my foster parents. They'd chosen fifteen year old Me a few months previously after Anita, my social worker, taking me away from the "Bankses" to their doorstep. It was unusual for a teenager to be permanently fostered. Looking back, they're terribly strenuous to be around, teenagers, with all those hormones and whatnot.

No, people usually wanted toddlers or preschoolers as far as I'd observed during my time in the home.

One just didn't pick a passive, lethargic looking, spotty teenager over a three year old bundle of smiles that emitted a smell of biscuits. But Phoebe and Greg *had.* They had explained that, with their jobs, they didn't have time for a small child that wasn't able to care for itself, get It's own breakfast or find It's way to school, but that they missed the company and the joy of a child and having to care about something at least a bit other than one another. Later I had realized that they simply weren't able to have one. It had been a rather warm day, very warm as a matter of fact.

As if summer was sensing it's nearing end and was giving a final moan, a final wave of warmth and sunshine before giving in to autumn's dismalness and clammy, creeping coldness.

And I'd been terribly bored, as I so often had been recently.

I'd been lying on the living room carpet, a cloth I had held under cold water draped over my face, listening to the sound of the television.

"No homework today?" Phoebe had asked mockingly with a hint of sincerity lingering in her voice. She was of such kind nature, but very serious about education, work and contribution to society. ("Young people never vote nowadays! Why do young people never vote?")

"Mmh," my answer had been.

"I don't know what to say, Lynette, sometimes your statements are so deep I'm speechless."

"I know."

"Are you stuck?"

"No, only have to do French but it's so effing warm!"

"Exuse me? Was that a bad word I heard coming from the TV?"

I'd blushed and smiled in a way that was meant to demonstrate my state of embarrassment. Having spent many years in different homes with different families that were more interested in the financial benefits of fostering than in me, I suppose I'd had no choice but to take to swearing. The fosterers and social workers *had* seen to us. We'd been fed, cleaned and all that, but they hadn't sat down with each and every one of us with a cup of hot chocolate - like a real, actual mum or dad would - after receiving a call from the headmaster, to casually work in things like how to verbally express oneself in an appropriate manner into a conversation. Or how to behave, and the trouble it could get you into if you didn't.

Birth control 'n stuff.

Did they? They did in a movie I'd seen once. I'd watched it with Al because, well, it was on and had decided in some part of my subconscious that it would probably be reasonable to remember this strategy when we, *if* we were to have kids as soon as they became horrid preteens.

"Look at that." Said Greg, who'd been quietly reading his newspaper.

He had half ascended from his chair, the approach of a smile on his face.

On the terrace, a red squirrel was playfully running after a small bird I couldn't identify, which proceeded to fly about it in a provocative manner.

After observing the animals for another moment, Greg got up, reached for the camera on one of the jam-packed bookshelves and took a picture. "Probably won't turn out… scampering about too much! You try, Lynni, you'll get them from a better angle down there."

"Mmh." I hadn't yet begun or even tried to fathom quiet, easily excited Greg running around taking pictures of (just about) literally everything and anything.

"C'mon, they'll be gone in a minute!"

I removed the cloth and rolled onto her side, then carefully picked up the Camera and looked through it. I followed the playful movement of the two creatures for a moment until it looked worth eternalizing. I took two shots before they moved to a part of the garden beyond my field of vision.

"Come on, Sweetheart. I admit that French was far from being my best subject but I know some things here and there."

"Just a second!"

The snow-white, hazy clouds with the clear blue sky in the background had something so idyllic about them; I impulsively got up off the carpet and went outside.

Five shots of five different formations later I returned inside to a proudly smiling Greg.

Even though the skin around his eyes was starting to wrinkle and his hair and stubble was graying, those blue eyes of his looked so young and eager. "It should be full of pictures soon, then we can get them developed and see if they're any good."

Sending in the film and, two weeks later, returning to the drug-store to find an envelope full of pictures with my name on it filled me with an unprecedented sensation of profound satisfaction.

Except for the slightly blurry photos of the squirrel chasing the bird, they had turned out nicely.

I soon discovered that some things, such as cloud formations or panoramic landscapes couldn't be captured exactly the way I saw them. That is, not without the proper equipment. And so, I began saving my monthly allowance, asking for specific objectives for my approaching birthday and Christmas, and had soon acquired a certain level of general knowledge and skill. I'll admit I wasn't that modest, in fact I found those skills pretty great. They were there alright, but I had *a lot* much to learn.

Though I would have loved to more than anything, I would never leave Fife until my mid-twenties (Al ad I would spend two very rainy weeks in Wales). I already pictured myself as a famous photographer taking shots for one of those educational magazines or something, of exotic country sides, people and creatures.

Still, I managed to capture more and more stunning images of regional country sides, people and animals, some of which made it into the school paper that appeared once a month. It was, as you can imagine, yet more squirrels and small birds and clouds more than anything, but it was a start.

By the time I was sixeen, I knew exactly what I wanted to do with my life, and as I was very aware of my own inner strength, I was sure nothing would get in my way.

Boy was I full of melodramatic rubbish at sixteen...

Lynne, 2015

Cam was already there and had what appeared to be some caramel latte or other in front of her. She looked up from her mobile phone and grinned when I sat – or rather flopped - down on the chair opposite with a noisy sigh of relief.
"Long day, eh?"
"You can say that again." I said as I picked up the card that listed hot and cold drinks and snacks.
"Started moving stuff round a bit in the shop, which I should have done ages ago. Dust and spiders everywhere. Starting to wonder what I'm paying Miles for!"
The waiter passed their table for the third time without looking in our direction.
"Er, excuse me? I'd like a plain mug of coffee please."

"Oh, come on." Cam interjected and drained her latte. "Order something you fancy! My treat! I'll have another one of these, please. And the chocolate fudge cake."

I felt myself blushing. "But I quite like just plain coffee."

"Should I come back in a few minutes?" The young man asked while writing down Cam's order.

"Make it two of each."

"But it's so…"

I made a gesture as if to strangle Cam as I felt myself go a deeper shade of red after the waiter had moved on.

"So what? Much? Come on Sweetheart, there's nothing on you!"

"I know, but all the trans fats, refined sugar and all that…trying to live healthier and stuff."

Cam looked at me sceptically as she spooned the cold remains of foamed milk from her cup.

"Expensive!" I whined. I held the card close to my friend's face, rather to make a point than anything else. "Five twenty-five for a cup of lukewarm effing milk? I could live off that for a week!"

I hid my own face behind the card in embarrassment. I had failed to maintain the illusion that money was no big issue. I lowered it quickly when the waiter arrived with the drinks and announced that the cake would be there in a minute.

"We don't go out that often. Got to have a treat now and again. Look at me, pigging out while I'm on low carb!

But without at piece of what's coming towards us right now life wouldn't be worth living."

Cam rubbed her hands together in delight as a big chunk of devil's food was placed before her.

"They make a mean chocolate cake here, and look, it comes with ice cream *and* whipped cream!"

It smelled bloody effing good. My mouth was watering. "I know. Thanks." Damn it, that hadn't come out as genuinely as I'd hoped. Would Cam nitpick or would she let it go?

"Is it really going that bad at the moment, Sweetheart?"

She had to nitpick. Of course she had to nitpick. She was the nitpicky-est nitpicker in…everywhere.

But she was my dear nitpicky friend Cam. And so, I looked up from my cake – it *was* a bloody mean cake indeed – and told her the truth about my financial situation.

Cam listened with sympathy in her big brown eyes and then gazed into the distance, deep in thought, while recommencing to eat her cake.

I looked around awkwardly and stirred my latte unnecessarily.

Cam finally spoke. "Have you considered maybe giving up the shop – no, let me finish – and staying in the business, but as an employee, like in an advert company or something, make a name for yourself and then go back to being your own boss with your own studio and all that? Imagine, people queuing up for you! Or even taking pictures of fashion models for magazines!" Cam's eyes glowed as if she were picturing herself strutting up and down the catwalk.

I thought about it for a minute. "But it's my dream. *That* filthy, come down little shop is my dream." I cringed when I said it out loud.

I sounded like a whiney child that was upset because It's parents told It that It simply couldn't open It's own ice cream shop right now.

"I know sweetheart." I could tell Cam could only just resist licking the remains off her plate. So could I. But when one was in their thirties there were things one should give one's best to resist, I decided, and put my plate back down.

"But think about it, are you making any money whatsoever of that dream of yours right now? You just told me about your problems. You've sold your jewelry, for God's sake. You're going without internet and a phone at home and everything. You've been wearing that tee for what, six years? You're *not* eating properly...You should be investing the little money you have in some proper food than in cigarettes!"

I wrapped my fleece around myself subconsciously to hide my skinniness. I'd always been lean. Now I didn't like to look in the mirror because I considered myself sort of ill looking. And old. But latter was probably the cigarettes. I'd never understood why Cam made such a fuss about her physique. She always spoke of herself as "chubby" or "just a bit too much". I found her curvy and feminine and gorgeous.

I realized I'd been daydreaming while gawping at her chest and nodded to show that I'd heard what she'd said. "I know. I'll think about it. It is a good idea."

"Please do. In the meantime, please say if you need some money to eat or something to wear or you want to use my internet to set up a website or whatever. I know you're uncomfortable with things like that, but you know I'm always there. You could even-" she leaned forward when she said this and looked at me with her serious-face so that I'd listen and take it in. "get out of that pokey flat and like with me."

I nodded reluctantly. I loved Cam, but I'd grown up fighting my own battles and had never known such genuine kindness, except during the time I'd spent with Greg and Phoebe.

And my time with Al. I shook off the thoughts as I felt tears of anger work their way towards my eyes and finished my coffee. "Thanks."

She looked at me thoughtfully. "You *are* off the booze though, aren't you?"

I blushed, even though I had no reason to feel guilty. I'd been dry for months.

"Of course. Besides, I couldn't afford it even if I wanted to." I laughed awkwardly and looked down muttering a "sorry" when she raised her eyebrows. She was not amused. Which I could understand. Cam had seen me in a rather dark place more than once and didn't want me back there. Neither did I, really, for that matter.

"Good. Keep it that way." She looked at her watch. "I've got to go."

"Where?"

"Meeting someone."

Now Cam was blushing. Cam didn't blush. And I caught the glimpse of a sheepish smile.

I thought. And something else, but I couldn't exactly figure out what.

"Who?" I asked slyly.

"Oh no one. Well, just a guy. Nothing serious. Just a casual dinner. Want to shower and change first, get some fresh make-up on. I'd have done that for you but had to work."

That was a rather vague description for the events that were to occur when she went out with "a guy" to be coming from Cam.

She usually got to listen to who the guy was, how serious it was, where they were going for dinner and how she'd keep topping his glass up and what very expensive and transparent piece of clothing she was going to change into.

This had to be serious. Or Cam was just getting more careful about men after she'd been repeatedly disappointed and had bawled her eyes out over tubfuls of cookie-dough ice cream or otherwise having to climb out some window in the middle of the night to get a taxi home.

"Have fun then." I said and smiled as I got up to hug her. "And thanks for the coffee. And everything."

Alan, 1998

Lunch was a disaster. Why did school lunches always have to be a disaster? Cooking was the easiest thing in the world.

Then again, I looked around the cafeteria and failed to count the number of pupils and teachers, there were a lot of people. Still, there wasn't really anything one could mess up about spaghetti with tomato sauce.

"Did you do the maths homework?" my mate Peter asked between two mouthfuls.

"I tried, was too bloody difficult. My mum and dad were too busy in the restaurant this week to help."

"Aw, damn."

"Why don't you do it yourself for once? You've got the stay at home mum and the time and all that."

"But homework's rubbish! I've got better stuff to do. Like football practice. We had two games at the weekend."

"Amazing."

"Hey!"

We were completely different types of people, Pete and I. He was so chatty, so enthusiastic. Most of all about football. I didn't fancy football very much at all. I watched a game here and there with my Dad, of course. When my Dad was home. He and Mum were usually in their restaurant, as was I. Partly because that was how I earned my pocket money, partly because I loved being there with the smells and sounds and people. It wasn't a fancy-dancy place. It was casual, just somewhere families went on a Friday night to avoid cooking – they had crayons, high-chairs and everything – or a group of mates would come for a pint after work.

"I've not got practice tonight, mind you. Can we go to your parents place for some chips after school?"

"Doesn't your mum cook?"

"Yeah, but she's out with my dad later on, some anniversary or other. They've always got the sports channel running there, haven't they? Al?"

I'd noticed noises that didn't fit in with the hectic, monotone murmur going through the cafeteria coming from a few tables away.

"Give it back! Please!"

"Take it back then, Fatty, come on!"

"It's my lunch-money! I'm hungry!"

"We're just trying to protect you from yourself getting any bigger, Fatty!"

It was Camilla Lawson, a girl from two forms below ours and was always being bullied because of her chubbiness.

"Should we do something?" Pete asked gingerly.

I'd already half gotten up. Maybe they were just messing with her and would give the money back. Idiots. That bloody Harvey Whatever He Was Called was about twice her size! Round the way, not up the way. Well, both, now that I looked more closely. He was the kind of pig that would make audible comments on female pupil's "racks" or the size of male teacher's metaphorical "balls" whenever they'd start a lesson, especially if the topic was poetry- or art-related.

"Right, how about you just bloody well back off, fat-face." Another girl had gotten up. It was that new girl, Lydia? Something like that. She was skinny and tall, and very pretty. People said she was living with Mr. Baker, the English teacher. Yvette?

One of the bullies was coming towards her.

"And how about you shut your face, dipshit."

"Not going to happen. I'm getting a teacher."

That wouldn't scare them. Nobody got teachers. Otherwise you were a Clipe.

"You're a bloody clipe then, wee shite. Is that what you want to be?"

"I'd rather be a clipe than a bloody fat arsehole."

She was staring him down. She meant it.

I felt myself blush. I'd have gotten up eventually, sure. But I'd have been more likely to have him beat me up than to get a teacher.

"Fuck you, little shithead." The Alpha-Bully spat at her eventually and thrust the five pound note back at Camilla.

Camilla said something to the other girl, it looked like a thank you. And the two went to get their lunch together.

I sat back down. Pete was talking again but I wasn't quite taking it in. I was – I had to admit to myself – sort of in awe of that girl. I looked in her direction one last time and then turned back to Pete. "Sorry, what?"

"I was asking if you could get your parents to switch to football if they've got rugby or something running?

Lynne, 1998

It was about two months before Greg and Phoebe were meant to sign the documents that would make them my real, actual legal guardians. My *parents*.

I was over the moon as were they.

And then the phone rang. Of course, the phone had to ring.

After a very serious sounding half hour conversation, Phoebe called us both to the kitchen table, poured us some tea and, dabbing her eyes delicately with a tissue, she declared nervously that her mother had been diagnosed with a kidney disease and was on dialysis. As there were no other living relatives, except for Phoebe's younger sister who lived abroad, and the old Mrs. Harris "detested" hospitals, Phoebe felt it was her obligation to take her in. She said this in a way that made me feel sure that Phoebe's mum had made it very clear that she was to feel just that. But Phoebe was clearly in shock about the bad news, so I let it go.

"Lynne won't mind sleeping on that big comfy couch for a bit, will you?" Greg gave me a one armed squeeze and a reassuring smile. He must have interpreted my expression as the fright of having worked out that I'd have to move out of my room for a while. That I didn't mind. It was all still absolute heaven compared to other homes where I'd never had so much as the bathroom mirror to myself or a say in what there would be for tea.

No, I'd just figured out that that this Mrs. Harris, Phoebe's mum, was about to become something like my grandmother. I embraced the fact with mixed feelings. But then, I'd been in and out of homes, meeting new people my whole life. And if she'd participated in producing and brought forth an endearing person such as Pheobe, she couldn't possibly be anything but sweet. Could she?

I ate my turkey sandwich in silence as I watched for Greg's car. He would be back with Mrs. Georgina Harris just shortly.
Phoebe had tried to get the day off but the no one could step in that day, as the flu was going round and the number of teachers at her school was currently rather wanting. Thus, I hoped Greg wouldn't be his easily-excited-but-quiet self the next few days and take over Phoebe's role of keeping his mother-in-law occupied. I was no good at that small-talk thing.

I shoved the rest of my sandwich into my mouth and made to get my jacket and boots when I saw them pull up in the driveway.

Outside, I saw Greg help a small figure bundled up in shawls and scarves right up to its nose.

He backed away, gesturing apologetically a second later as if he'd been shooed.

As they walked up the short path up to the front door, he still walked right beside her, commenting on the cold weather in a humorous way, his hands out of his pockets so as to be ready to catch her if she did stumble.

I swallowed and put a smile on my face as the approached and came to a halt.

"Georgina, this is Lynette-"

"Who's this?"

"Lynette. Lynne. Phoebe and I-"

"Another one of those, eh? After that David

boy going off to school with a hundred quid a week to buy cigarettes and booze?"

I felt my smile fade and the hand I'd held out to her go slightly limp, but I pulled myself together. This was Phoebe's mum. Maybe she had a really dark humor?

"Georgina, that was something different entirely. David was a nice boy, we were just not right for each other. Now, will you take Georgina inside and put the kettle on, Lynni? I'll get the luggage."

"Don't you dare drop anything! There's jewelry in there that was more expensive than that ancient car of yours!"

I don't know if I imagined it, but I think Greg, while still smiling cheerfully, lifted his eyebrows imperceptibly as he turned to walk back down the path.

"Take this." Georgina said without so much as glancing at me as she handed me her jacket. "Put it up there."

I wanted to say something, had to say something, but was worried that no more than an embarrassing stutter would emerge that would make me look as thick as this woman seemed to want to think I was.

I couldn't recall ever having felt this way before. Not since I'd given up on making an effort with my foster families. But things were different with Greg and Phoebe and I would hate myself forever if I messed things up by saying the wrong things.

"W-would you like a seat?"

"I've been sitting for the past three hours. No, I do not want a seat."

"Alright."

She simply stood and looked around critically, at the pictures hanging in the walls of the hallway, the decorations, the color of the walls.

I left her to it and briskly walked to the kitchen to put the kettle on and get some cups out.

I wondered whether Mrs. Harris – I didn't feel quite comfortable thinking of her as Georgina just yet - would prefer it if I got out the good china, but decided I'd rather not touch something so delicate.

"Here we are."

I heard Greg huff and put the suitcases down with a thump.

"Wouldn't you rather go into the living room? Have a sit down? I'll get some shortbread out."

"Why does everyone want me to sit? I might be ill but I'm not exactly dead just yet."

"Well..."

Poor Greg. I moved back closer to the hallway as I felt his discomfort almost as painfully as my own.

"I'm dying for a cup of tea, and it would be nice if you would join us."

Greg was handling this in a manner I could only dream of imitating. Then again, he must have endured her a number of times so far and wasn't in shock as I was just now.

"Still take yours black, Georgina?"

"Good and strong. Not that lukewarm water you make."

Greg did make weak tea, but I liked it better that way. When I left the teabag in too long it made me feel sort of dehydrated.

"When's Phoebe going to be here?"

I wondered whether Mrs. Harris felt as uncomfortable in our presence as I did in her's right now. I too caught myself glancing at the clock, longing for the sound of the front door being unlocked.

"She should be here in just over an hour. In time to take you to your dialysis-appointment."

Greg handed her a cup of steaming, syrupy tea and I briefly thought I registered the suggestion of a nod, a polite, silent thank you.

She caught me observing her and I felt myself colour as I smiled and looked away reflexively.

"Don't talk very much, do you."

It was a statement, not a question.

"It depends." I was at a complete loss for words.

"Yes." She said, her tone more than a tad deprecatory, looking me up and down.

"Would you like me to talk?"

"It would be polite to make conversation seeing as I'm going to be living here and my daughter has taken you in."

"Now, Georgina, Lynne's just having a quiet day, eh Lynni? She's just fine."

Greg rubbed my back, having sensed that Mrs. Harris had made me slightly uncomfortable having had taken on the kind of tone she had.

I was starting to suspect my theory must be wrong. She didn't have a very dark humor.

It was just after three when Phoebe arrived. After greeting Greg and me with a brief hug and a kiss on the cheek each, she approached her mother and embraced her carefully. "Mummy!" She exclaimed then, with a slightly awkward undertone. Her extraordinary broad smile didn't look real. I tried to guess what kind of relationship they'd had when Phoebe had been my age and younger as I made to gather the empty cups, so they didn't feel like I was invading a private mother-daughter-reunion moment.

Could such an assertive, pugnacious personality be purely congenital?

I wondered what the late Mr. Harris had been like and what Phoebe had felt like towards him as I filled the kettle up again as Phoebe would surely like a cup before they set off for the appointment, but mostly to have something to do while they talked.

I quickly tried to ban the thought of Mr. and Mrs. Harris naked and tangled up together, losing all control of their facial expressions that were contorted in passion. Phoebe and her sister hadn't popped up out of nowhere, after all. Maybe they were adopted?

"When are you going to stop this nonsense, picking up children off the street?"

I heard Mrs. Harris say. She didn't so much as try to lower her voice.

And there went my theory that Mrs. Harris was a virgin.

"Oh, mum. Don't worry about that. Lynnette's great. She's so nice and so bright. We're planning on adopting her, you know."

Phoebe had said this with an audibility that was clearly meant to reach my ears. I supposed she was worried that I could be hurt by Mrs. Harris words.

"Adopt?"

"Yes. Adopt. We're very excited."

"What kind of background does this girl have?"

It was like I could hear Phoebe's anxiety through the silence. She lowered her voice when she answered this time. "She did have a difficult childhood. Mother was a terrible drug addict and earned her money in ways that are…well… often considered as a last resort.

Poor woman.

Lynne was taken away by the social services and in and out of families from the age of five."

It was difficult to hear over the sound of the kettle. I realized that I shouldn't be listening anyway but adult's had been talking about me with hushed voices ever since I could remember and I'd decided long ago that I didn't like it. It always meant they were talking about what a difficult childhood I'd had (poor girl…), like Phoebe, or humph-ing that *I* was bound to be difficult, like Mrs. Harris. It wasn't like it was a big secret I wasn't allowed to know about. I knew the details of the first years of my life better than anybody. I'd felt the pain, I'd had seen and heard the things a child should be protected from.

"I don't care how difficult her childhood was, I'll still not hesitate to call the police if I find any of my belongings so much as two inches from where I've placed them myself."

Ben, 2015

I was hungry. Thirsty. Tired, cold, wet.

I'd been in that same state for about a week. Well, one and a half days.

Two more bloody months and it would all have been over. I would have been free to make my own way. In a half way home or something at first of course, but still. Free.

The act of running away had been so impulsive and bloody effing stupid.

But I'd forgiven myself seen as how I'd had to put up with abuse from the other kids since I could remember.

A woman dumped her half-eaten sausage roll in the bin next to the bench I'd been sitting on the past few hours. Jackpot!

I looked around to check there was no one watching. I was a bit embarrassed sticking my hand into the bin to get someone else's food out. But hey, I was a growing teenager and I was hungry! Also, I'd eaten bugs when I was little before my mum had stopped me. So I wasn't really picky about what went in my mouth. I grinned like an idiot and inwardly slapped my forehead when I realized how dirty that sounded.

It was still warm and she'd only had one bite.

I just about swallowed it whole it was so good! My stomach was still grumbling audibly though.

This was a good place to sit. It was near a play park, and during the day I supposed a lot of schoolkids would come by or parents with small children and would have something or other – the odd banana or half-crushed chocolate bar – they'd throw away.

At night, I could huddle up in the nearby bushes or under a slide like the night before. It wasn't too cold yet. It was September I think. Still cold as shit, mind.

I hadn't worked out yet what I would do when it got colder. I hadn't worked out what was going to happen at all yet, really. All I knew was: I was most likely officially a missing person by now, I was a bloody mess and probably smelt like something decaying, I had about two more hours before I'd have to move, otherwise people would get suspicious of me perching here, looking like shit day after day or the police came here to look for me.

I had seriously considered going to a busier place and begging or maybe even get myself cleaned up and find a job at a super market or something. But both of these were no option, really. I had no cv that showed I was worth giving a chance, and social workers would have me back home or – as I'd most likely not be wanted anymore – at another home before I could explain a thing and who knew what awaited me there.

Still, I thought as I wrapped my jacket tighter around me, maybe it was the best place for me to be right now. What was the worst that could happen if I just went back? Or went to the police myself, as I probably couldn't be shouted at *too* loud by Thomas and Judith or Sandra if I turned up at the home in their presence.

I sort of wanted to cry.

But I was nearly sixteen. And I hadn't cried for a very long time. I'd learnt not to.

Lynne, 2015

I was drenched. Why had I had to wear a white shirt? I tried pathetically to hide the stains by keeping my elbows pressed to my sides as I handed took the handful five pound notes from the mother of the baby I'd just spent half an hour wrestling.

"And can I order some of these picture frames. Three of the small ones for the mantelpiece and the big one."

"Alright, I should have them round about when the pictures are edited and developed next week. I'll give you a call when it's all ready to be collected." I hesitated before slowly asking "Would you like the photo's to be edited?"

"If you find it to be necessary, I'm sure you…know what you're doing." The woman looked me up and down while rocking her squealing baby, Jamie. Did baby's still tend to puke a lot at that age?

"Alright, well" I scribbled on my notebook. "Would you prefer the stainless steel frames or the dark wood ones?"

The woman considered both models, releasing the child with one hand to touch them.

I felt awkward with my sweaty shirt and messy hair, beside this expensive looking woman. About my age, maybe a bit older, blonde hair luxuriously falling around her shoulders like silk, shiny, heavy looking earrings dangling from her ears. I had blonde hair too, but I'd dyed it myself again and again and it was sort of frizzy and you could see the roots. I touched it self-consciously.

"I must say I prefer the wood, the stainless steel is very stylish and modern but it has an old fashioned, homely flair to it. Sort of retro."

"Yes, retro." She was still considering and touching the frames, but I could almost feel her look me up and down again. And then, as if my statement had helped her make up her mind "I'll go for the stainless steel." She managed to unzip her purse elegantly by pushing out her hip to stop Jamie from slipping down any further. He seemed to find her left earring very interesting, they were so shiny he'd probably discovered his reflection in it.

"That makes sixty pounds then." I said as I wrote down the order. "I'll throw in the third small frame as a gift. What name should I write down?"

She looked up, seemingly pleasantly surprised. "Oh. Thank you. Smith. Maria

Smith. Outch, Jamie, not Mummy's earring, outch!" she squealed.

Jamie let the earring, that he'd started tugging at, go abruptly and his lower lip started to tremble before his eyes filled with tears and he let out a long wail.

"Oh, not now."

I reached into the drawer where I kept the sweets for kids that had had their picture taken or needed occupation while their parents did. It had been Miles' idea. He'd also organized some children's books and a puppet from a second-hand-shop. He was better at that kind of thing.

"Kiddo" I attempted to get his attention. "Jamie, look what I've got!" I held out a packet of chocolate buttons. "Is he allowed?" I asked Maria. I'd remembered to late that some parents didn't allow sweets before a meal or at all a few times and had left the mothers with an even more upset child than before after they'd had a packet of buttons or a biscuit held in front of their face.

"Yes, if that stops him crying. Look Jamie, you like chocolate buttons."

The tears stopped and a smile spread across the round face as he reached out his hands for the chocolate.

"There, that's better." Maria Smith looked at me gratefully. "Thank you, once this one starts..." She rolled her eyes theatrically. "Do you have children?"

"I..." I ruffled my hair, making it even messier in the process. Very briefly, I didn't know whether I was blushing or going pale. Then I regained my composure. "No. No I don't."

Maria Smith seemed briefly irritated by my sudden nervousness. "That's a shame, you seem to be good with them. Anyway, we'll be on our way. See you next week."

"Have a nice day, I'll be sure to give you a call about the photos, I think we've got some nice ones."

With a smile and a now very chocolaty child, she left the shop and while the door was still dropping shut, Miles pushed it back open and entered, followed by Cam.

"Wow Miles, only fifteen minutes late! That must be you record!"

Had that come out too mean?

"Sorry, M'am! I'll make sure it's only ten tomorrow!"

"Do you even take me seriously?"

"Sir, yes, Sir!" and then "Of course I do, Lynne." He smiled apologetically as he dropped his rucksack in the corner and removed his coat.

"Someone has had to leave at "Bigg's", kid hurt itself at playschool or something, so it wasn't easy to get away."

He looked tired and hadn't shaved. It suited him. The unshaven part I mean.

"Don't worry, just messing with you. Make yourself a coffee or have a cigarette and then come inside, got some orders for frames to make and bills and stuff."

"Look at the poor boy, he needs a break," Cam put out her lip and gave me her puppy eyes.

"So do I, Love. No one pouts for me and says "poor Lynne, she needs a break.""

"Oh, don't we all." She unbuttoned her coat and sat in her settee. "Can I get a coffee too?"

"You won't get one of your fancy lattes or cappuccinos here though."

There was no need to throw a wink or anything of the sort in with Cam. She got it.

"Biscuit?"

"Not unless you've brought any."

"Not even a bloody rich tea biscuit for your old pal, pff!"

"Early Christmas presents for the customers, eh?" Miles had returned with three cups of coffee that neither matched in shape nor in size and was looking over the orders.

"No Miles, you know we give away 90-pound gift vouchers and sets of china just a few days before Christmas."

It took him a minute, but he grinned and shook his head in amusement.

"Or is this a mistake?"

"No Miles. I'm knackered as hell but still quite capable of doing simple maths, thank you very much."

Cam, obviously sorry for Miles having to put up with mean, sarcastic Me, came to his rescue. "I think Lynne's trying to get in the customer's good books by throwing in a little something here and there. Just a little marketing strategy I think, is it?" She winked knowingly as she put the "I hate Mondays" mug to her lips.

"Yup. We'll see how and if it works."

Miles looked the orders over once more, impressed. "If it doesn't end up costing us more in the end, that's great."

He had a point. Damn. We'd already given in and lowered our prices.

"Well, we'll see. We can't be picky or tight at the moment anyway."

He looked down and nodded, the line between his thick, dark brows growing deeper.

He looked up and caught me watching him. I looked away, embarrassed. "Miles, if you've got time during the next few days, would you mind doing a bit of renovating round the entrance? Looks a bit come down."

"If it doesn't rain, why not."

"Thanks."

He picked up the phone and got to work and Cam, who'd been scrolling on her smart-phone, got up and stood close beside me. "Look at this," she said as she held the phone in front of me so I could see, her voice somewhere between a whisper and a squeak. "Isn't it *fab?*"

I took it to get a closer look. It was a blouse, navy blue, with a price ticket still on. Slightly transparent with little bundles of sequins and pearls the same colour as the fabric sewn on here and there.

"Going out again tonight with *the guy* or just treating yourself?" I nudged her playfully.

She suddenly looked…guilty? Nervous? "Both… I was thinking this with the black trousers and the dark-blue-ish pumps, you know the ones? They're quite high but we won't be walking a lot or anything." I sniggered inwardly.

"It's nice." I wasn't really the right person to ask about whether something was suitable to wear on a date or anywhere else, she was the professional designer after all, but my answer had been genuine. It looked nice. Cam-ish.

For some reason she looked like she was trying to find the right words, or something to say at all. "Should I wear a black top or something underneath? Think it would be too slutty on it's own? It's quite see-through." I knew Cam was a rambler, but not a nervous one that got anxious whenever a silence occurred that lasted longer than five seconds. I couldn't help but wonder if something was wrong.

"Depends." I looked up to check that Miles was still on the phone negotiating with our supplier. "Do you just want *you know what* or is it more a serious thing?"

She shrugged. "Don't know yet. But I quite like him."

"You quite like a lot of people. You're choice, it's nice either way."

"Thanks, it really caught my eye. Along with about fifteen other things, but this did it for me in the changing room."

She lowered her phone and looked up at me. "When do you think you'll try and, you know, get back on the horse and all that?"

Her question caught me by surprise. That was something I hadn't given a second of thought yet. "I really don't know, I…suppose I'm just not ready or…I don't know."

For once, she didn't probe any further and dropped the subject, suddenly embarrassed. "Sorry, Love."

She got up. "Do you mind if I go to the loo? I'm bursting!"

"Go ahead, you know where it is."

Miles had finished his phone call and was writing something down, probably the dates he was told the frames would arrive on so that we could phone the customers.

"You know what's really interesting about you, Lynne?"

"No, but I suppose you're going to tell me."

He sniggered in his boyish way. He often looked so worn out I forgot how young he was.

"You swear, like, all day long. Cunt this, effing that. And yet, while not swearing, I've only ever heard you refer to the act of coitus or genitals as *you know what* or *it*." I blushed violently. He had a point. Why did I do that?

"Sex. Coitus. Intercourse." There you go. Happy?"

He raised his hands and laughed in an "It's not like I made you!"-way.

"What are you eavesdropping for anyway?"

"Does it have something to do with the way you were brought up?"

I considered this theory for a moment. None of the fosterers I'd had had ever approached me in the attempt to have *the talk,* as they say.

Maybe they should have.

"I'll give it some thought."

He seemed content with the answer, as he smiled and continued what he had been doing.

Something vibrated on the armrest of the settee Cam had been sitting in. I glanced at her phone reflexively and, after taking a step towards the shelf where I'd put my cup, took another look just to be sure. Alan Johnson.

Al.

Cam returned from the toilet.

"Bit constipated, are you?"

"No, I've just been needing to go since this morning, thank you very much. No time at work for any physical needs or any such nonsense." She pursed her lips and raised her eyebrows meaningfully, apparently imitating her boss.

"Traitor."

Her face went blank. "What?"

"You heard me, traitor."

"Wh…"

I laughed awkwardly. "Going to Alan's place for a meal tonight, are you? He just called, better give him a ring incase it's because of the reservation or something."

I wasn't good at interpreting facial expressions and things like that, but had that been relief on Cam's face just there?

"I'll do that. Thanks. I'm going to get a move on, lovely to see you!"

Cam gathered her things, gave me a brief, one-armed hug and was out the door before I could even make my sarcastic comment "wasn't Al's a tad too "fish and chips and Guinness" for a glamorous night out?". Oh well. That was Cam, always on the run.

I downed my coffee and got back to work.

Lynne, 1998

I'd tried on three different combinations of tops and trousers, then my plain blue dress – it was still fairly warm after all, though it was bound to get cooler later on – and then decided it was best if I stuck to my regular jeans and sweatshirt look. I gave my hair a comb and pulled it back, making sure no odd hairs stuck out. I needed to get some dye, dark roots were showing again.

Phoebe always kept running her fingers through my hair a few days after I'd freshly bleached it, asking "if I really had to do that? That my hair was bound to be lovely it's natural colour".

I just shrugged, not really knowing what to say. It wasn't that I wanted to be "in" or "cool", I thought it was just me. And Mrs.

Harris, she disapproved and made no effort whatsoever to hide it. Not that I cared.

I didn't wear make-up, that was one thing I didn't have to worry about. I'd tried it once and just ended up smudging it all over my face in a attempt to remove sticky-ness from my eyes because I'd forgotten it was there.

My stomach kept cramping up with excitement, though it wasn't an unpleasant sensation altogether.

It hadn't been there until about an hour ago.

I tried to recall how I'd felt when Al had asked me out the day before and smiled to myself.

I hadn't been expecting it, nor had I been hoping or waiting for it. I'd never really thought about *boys* or *dating* or who was *"hot"* or *not*, like a lot of others girls seemed to, to be honest.

My friend Cam was quite into Harry Fraser. She'd start to squeak excitedly if he was near by and looked like she was going to faint when he smiled at her in the cafeteria once.

He seemed nice enough, I supposed.

I'd been asked once if I liked girls by a few girls in my class, after they'd spent a minute or two throwing glances in my direction and whispering. They hadn't meant it in a mean way, I don't think so anyway. I didn't see why something like that had to be discussed and speculated about endlessly. About two weeks later Jessica and Charlotte had outed themselves before the French lesson had started and it was subject number one for gossip for weeks until it was replaced by the rumor of Mr McCain snogging Miss Davis in the little hallway just after Room 104. I wasn't really interested in any of this, but it was hard to overhear the details.

Anyway, there I was, ready to go out with a boy for the first time in my life.

Al had come up to our table during lunch while Cam had gotten up to get pudding.

He'd stuttered a bit, then grinned and just said "hi", while looking at a spot between my tray and an old school paper at the edge of the table someone had apparently forgotten.

"Hi." I said back after swallowing my last mouthful of mashed potatoes. I presumed he was going to ask me if we were about to leave so that he could sit there or whether Cam was seeing someone. I'd seen him look in our direction every day during lunch for the past few months but hadn't bothered commenting it as I knew Cam fancied Harry and he didn't mind her either.

"Umm, can I sit down?"

"We'll be leaving in a minute, I'm just waiting for my friend."

"No, no, it's fine, I'll be off in a sec. I was just…I'm Alan. Alan Johnson." He held out his hand shyly. "Or Al, whatever you prefer."

"I'm Lynne." Soon-to-be Baker, I added in thought.

Alan Johnson. I liked his name. It sounded harmonic.

"I was just wondering if you'd like to…I mean, only if you want to…I don't know, go to the pictures after school tomorrow? Or for some fish and chips?"

I didn't realize I was just looking at him, my mouth open, for a few seconds.

He shifted awkwardly and his skin went blotchy.

"Or both. Or whatever you want. Or not."

I decided not to think too much about his offer. It couldn't hurt to get out and do something with someone other than Cam for a change, after all. And despite the fact that I loved Phoebe and Greg I wasn't keen on spending a lot of time at home currently. Except when Mrs. Harris was at dialysis or some other medical appointment or fast asleep.

I also decided spontaneously that I liked him, in one way or another. I didn't hate him. And nodded. "That would be nice."

His shoulders relaxed and he smiled. "Great. Oh, you could come to my parent's place, it's just round the corner of Bartlett Street, where that little Indian grocery shop is. You know where?"

I nodded once more. "I know. When? Six?"

"See you tomorrow at six then. I'll ask my dad to save us a table." He got up and added "I'm looking forward to it."

"Ready to go out with your boyfriend?" Phoebe teased when I left the bathroom and went past the kitchen to get my jacket and trainers on.

I'd had to tell her something as she'd just have to cook for the three of them that evening and had decided there was no reason to make something up. I was just going out for a fish supper with someone. I was glad Mrs. Harris was in her room having a nap before dinner, she was bound to make some unfriendly comment.

"Don't know about that, I'm ready to go out with some guy called Alan anyway."

She dried her hands and gave me a hug. A proper hug. "Have fun, Love. Don't be home too late."

She recommenced peeling carrots, as she was making some roast or other. She was a good cook but didn't often have time to prepare full meals.

"Phoebe?"

"Mh?"

"Can you...Would you mind not telling Mrs....your mum where I am?"

"Why? What's the matter?" I think she looked more concerned than irritated.

I looked away. "I feel like she despises me."

"Oh Lynne."

"I'm sorry. I just-" she hugged me once more, tightly this time.

"I know my mum can be very harsh. Trust me. You mustn't take it personally." She held my gaze when she caught my eyes to emphasize her words. "She's even more tense than usual with her illness making her feel unwell and having to live somewhere else and we've had young people live with us before that were very difficult and frightened her."

I hesitated, then nodded. I still wasn't sure. I couldn't imagine that woman being frightened by anything, never mind difficult, emotionally mixed-up teenagers.

"But if you don't want me to, of course I won't tell her. If she asks, I'll just say you're out with a friend."

Which I was as far as I was concerned. But Phoebe seemed to be convinced that this was a "date" with candles and holding hands and all that and delighted about it, so I didn't say anything.

I was glad I'd remembered to take my jacket. It wasn't really cold yet, but I could see my breath as a veil of fine, silvery mist when I exhaled.

Little John's wasn't far. About fifteen minutes walk. "Greg had come down the driveway just after I'd left the house, sneaked me a ten pound note and told me to get a taxi if I didn't feel comfortable walking home in the dark later on.

The front of the building that was in a row of other shops consisted of glass and there was a small pot plant on either side of the entrance.

And Alan was waiting, shifting on his feet to keep warm, his hands in the pockets of his trousers as if he didn't really know what to do with them.

Alan Johnson.

As I approached him I took a closer look at him. Dark hair, dark or maybe hazel-ish eyes, healthy complexion. Delicate but masculine features, average height and physique. And a tiny mole on the right side of his chin.

I came to a halt in front of him. "Hi."

"Hi."

Silence.

"Do you want to go inside?"

I nodded and went through the door when he held it open and gestured for me to enter.

The environment was modern but still homely and comfortable. Neither a place where you had to worry about not sitting upright enough nor where you had to worry about getting involved with drug-dealers or drunks. I'd seen both.

There were families, young couples, groups of school kids, one or two business men having a drink.

"My dad saved that table over here, is that alright?"

I nodded as I took my jacket off and sat down. The matching tables and chairs were dark wood, a bit like the one's in Phoebe's and Greg's dining room, but without the table cover. There was a screen near the bar where a sports channel was running.

A young man approached us. "Hi there Mate, not working tonight, eh?" he winked at Alan and nodded at me politely in greeting. "Nope." He gestured towards the young man. "Lynne, this is Ron, he works for my parents after Uni. This is Lynne, a friend from school."

"Friend, eh?" Ron winked meaningfully once more. "Nice to meet you. Can I get you something to drink?"

"A coke, please."

Ron got out his notebook. "One coke. And for you Al? Going to contain yourself tonight with the booze a bit though, aren't you?"

"A ginger beer should do the trick for now, thank you very much."

"Alright. I'll be right back."

"He's a bit mad, but he's fine." Alan said apologetically when Ron was out of earshot.

"That's alright." I said cheerfully. I didn't mind, I had that kind of humor some people considered mean or not very funny at all, it was good to hear comments like that from someone else for a change.

We got our drinks and ordered something to eat. Al had fish and chips, I ordered macaroni and cheese and covered it in brown sauce.

He looked at it with a raised eyebrow, then nodded approvingly and said "interesting combination, I'll have to give that a try."

We talked about the restaurant, the food, school, teachers. How old were we? Sixteen. Seventeen going on eighteen, he'd repeated a year.

Later on we had ice cream. Did I want to go to the cinema? No thanks, maybe next time. He smiled when I said this and nodded. "Next time, then."

We talked about ourselves, about the fact that I usually wasn't this talkative, no, neither was he. About my love for reading and photography, and his love for cooking and baking. How unusual for a boy. What could he cook? This and that, he learned a lot from his dad when he was here. (His mate Pete liked to call him a fanny when he dropped in spontaneously while he was making scones. Then he'd scoff five of them with jam, or rather the other way round.)

About our childhood. I caught myself going a bit quiet at this point but he seemed genuinely interested and so I started to talk and he listened.

When I took a minute to look around this time the atmosphere had changed as if by magic, like we'd been in our own little world for the past three hours.

The families with small children had left and been replaced with groups of adults that were drinking wine or Guinness with their meal, women gesturing enthusiastically while describing situations they'd encountered throughout the week and more people were sitting at the bar, watching the rugby game or laughing cheerfully at a comment one of them had made about a move of one of the players. I felt so comfortable and so un-like myself. Even more comfortable and eager to chat than with Cam, who usually did all the talking.

I turned to face Alan and caught him studying me. Not in a rude way, like people often did when sitting opposite to you on the train or bus without really noticing that made you feel really self-conscious. He looked away shyly for a moment, then looked back and smiled apologetically. I didn't mind him looking at me, it had been a kind sort of look. (Though a part in the back of my head inevitably shouted "what are you gawking at, you cunt?")

I felt a tingling sensation in the pit of my stomach and wondered whether I was getting ill.

I didn't really get ill very often but two people in my class had had to leave school that week with sickness and diarrhea.

But it didn't feel like I was about to puke.

Then I wondered if it was this feeling Cam always described when she talked about Harry Fraser. He'd pushed his empty bowl to the side and laid both his hands on the table and was playing with a toothpick he'd unwrapped. I felt the urge to reach across and touch them, even though I wasn't that crazy about physical contact.

Impulsive as I was, I did reflexively but pulled them away and clasped my hands under the table with a "sorry."

He laughed kindly and reached his hand out as an invitation for me to take it. I hesitated, then reached out and placed my hands in his. When my skin touched his it was like an electric shock, I drew in my breath sharply and hoped he hadn't noticed. His hands were slightly bigger than mine with long fingers and clean nails.

Later on, Alan walked me home and I decided I would give Greg his ten pounds back the next day.
His dad had managed to leave the kitchen for a minute to say hello. A tired looking but warm man in his early fifties, I'd guessed. I liked the place and the atmosphere and the people and I decided I'd be back, if not with Alan or to see Alan then perhaps with Phoebe and Greg. And Mrs. Harris, I supposed, inevitably. Or Cam.
We stood in silence for the best part of a minute when we arrived, like they often did in Hollywood movies I looked up at now and again while lying on the living room carpet with a book in the evening.

I did something unusual and broke the silence for a change. "I had a great time."

"Me too. See you on Monday."

He hesitated, as if considering saying something else, then leaned forward and gave me a brief, clumsy peck on the cheek before disappearing down the driveway.

Lynne, 2015

The pictures of Jamie Smith had turned out nicely. I'd expected most of them to be blurry as he had wriggled about quite a lot in the process, but I was positive that they would live up to the standards of Maria Smith.

He was smiling mischievously on each one, which seemed to underline the character of the toddler nicely. Not that this was a bad thing, he seemed to be a happy child, one that laughed more than pouted or cried, one that was content with small pleasures like a bag of chocolate buttons. I'd seen all types of children throughout my years in the home and in different households. Often had a lot to do with the parent's manners and ways of bringing up, but never everything. For instance, I thought, a woman like Maria Smith was bound to spoil her child, but as much as I could tell by the small glimpse caught at their life through the lenses of my camera, this didn't seem like the "I want!" type of child at all. But then again, one can't judge anyone properly before knowing them, really knowing them for a long time. Mostly anyway, if someone's downright horrible to the bone, you usually figure that out pretty quickly.

Miles was about to leave for his late shift at "Bigg's" and was clearing up the brushes he'd been using to paint the doorframe when a thought occurred to me.

"Miles, what do you actually *do*?"

He hesitated and looked at me wide eyed in incomprehension "wh..."

"I mean, apart from being my servant and working your arse off at Bigg's."

"Oh, I…" he continued clearing up and looked thoughtful for a moment. "I eat, I sleep a bit, throw in a shower now and then when the stink's unbearable." He winked.

"I go for a pint with mates, watch a fair bit of TV. Yeah…pretty much sums it up. Why?"

"You're not waiting to study or planning a big work and travel tour or anything like that? You make burgers and shower? How old are you?"

"Twenty-four and a half." He smiled playfully and patted himself on the shoulder like a kid that was very proud indeed of his advanced age of eight and three quarters.

It had been a quiet day and I was bored. And I realized I didn't know a single thing about the life of my only employee who at the same time was, though neither of us had ever said it out loud (him because I'd never dream of going all emotional and him because he probably didn't know), one of my only friends. So I decided it wouldn't kill me to have a go at an actual conversation.

"What would you do if you could choose?"

I'd sat down and was watching him. Watching his facial expressions change from neutral to questioning to thoughtful, watching the way he moved while clearing up, awkwardly scratching the back of his head and then nodding to himself as he remembered what he was wanting to do and finally relax and let himself drop on the chair beside the settee I'd claimed for myself. I didn't consider it rude to look at people. I didn't stare, I merely observed to get a picture of what someone might be like, what they might have endured. What other people found out by asking a lot of questions, I did this way, and it didn't seem to bother anyone. Words could lie, gestures, expressions and movements usually couldn't if one looked closely enough. And though I wasn't an expert on interpreting gestures and expressions, I still managed to get a feel for people by watching.

When Miles had seen the employment advert in the window and had come in for an "interview", I'd not sat down and asked him a lot of trick questions to see whether he was fit for the job, whether he'd stutter nervously when I asked him why I should employ him or what his strengths and weaknesses were. I'd offered him coffee, asked him to help me out for an hour and then told him he was fine and could start the next day. Though he tended to come a few minutes late now and then and was a bit of a klutz, I'd never regretted my choice.

"If I could choose. That's a good question. I mean I finished school and all that and had fairly good grades. Got my A-levels. But then my mum got ill and died when I was nineteen - yeah, pretty sad - and somehow it all just…" he made a gesture as if suggesting that something had tipped or simply gotten mixed up.

"Probably would have studied and become a social worker or a teacher. Both don't pay that well but I like people, I like kids, so…" he shrugged.

"Bloody well do it then, for God's sake."

He pretended to look offended. "What if I like it just fine here with you, and at Bigg's, and in my pokey little flat above the pub."

I got up and went to the door to light a cigarette.

"What would you do if you could choose? Would you be doing this?"

I nodded as I inhaled the smoke of the first drag.

"I'd be right here." I considered for a moment. "I'd like to get around more. Africa. South America. Scandinavia. Get some images worth capturing. Landscapes, people, animals, food…" I inhaled once more and Miles came to join me with his electric cigarette thingy. "Why don't you?"

"I don't really know. My Ex and…some other stuff and I suppose it just…" I made the same gesture he had to visualize his situation.

He nodded in comprehension. I loved him at that moment for not picking.

"And I suppose I feel like I just need to get this project…" I stroked at the dry, not yet re-painted part of the doorframe "well, needs to be seen to before I can start anything new. I need to try to get a few more regional clients before I fly off to Chile or Egypt.

"Seems reasonable to me. But I will think about what you said about the follow-your-dreams thing." His gaze was somewhere far away and I could tell he really meant it.

"Good."

I put out my cigarette in the rather full ashtray I'd placed at the side of the bottom doorstep where no one could see it if they weren't examining the area too closely.

"Anyway," he said. "I'll be off. See you tomorrow at two?"

I nodded and waved good-bye before going back inside to get my things.

I'd thought about the tip Cam had given me about the website and decided that I'd go to the internet café before I did my food shopping. And maybe, just maybe I'd have a look in the small electric shop near by to see what they had on offer and treat myself to a new laptop. It didn't have to be one of those fancy ones with a keyboard that changed colour and shit, but if I was going to expand even regionally, even *locally* I'd have to adapt to the way the modern society functioned. Very modern, very expensive society. I had one at the studio, but it was rather old and slow and all I had on it was a program to enable me to do my work, there was no internet. I had an E-Mail address, but that was about it.

Cam had offered more than once to lend me the money, internet, and once or twice even to move in with her. Greg and Phoebe had offered the same. And Al and Al's parents.

But I didn't want to hear anything about it. Every time a small part of me had said "go on you big bloody idiot, it's fine, you need it!" or "go on, what a laugh it would be living with Cam? That would stop you sulking about your stinky little studio apartment" but I couldn't, simply couldn't bring myself to reach out and take it. I'd often considered just grabbing the few things I owned and moving into the studio…that currently seemed to be the best temporary option. At least I'd have a bloody phone.

It was eight minutes past five and already getting dark.

I didn't have the slightest clue about computers or laptops other than how to transfer photos from a camera to a laptop and do some basic airbrushing, but perhaps the guy at the internet café could help me. If not, surely Cam or Greg or Miles could explain one thing or the other about setting up a website and things like that.

I had to pass the park to get to the shops, Al's place - "Little John's" - and a row of toy-, clothes- and tourist shops. My weekly trip to get some fresh food got me a bit of exercise at least.

I passed "Little John's". Was Cam and her boyfriend or lover or whoever this mysterious man was there already? Or was she still getting dolled up?

I carefully peered inside, praying that Al was in the kitchen or somewhere at the back where he wouldn't catch me gawking and, more importantly, I wouldn't see him.

A few people having an early dinner or a late lunch or just cake, but no Cam, and no stunningly handsome, mysterious man under forty who appeared to be looking out for someone.

My stomach rumbled when I saw a big plate of chips being placed in the center of a group of teenagers and the almost audible munching and ketchup pouring had begun, and thus decided to get everything done quickly so I could go home and have a cheese and pickle sandwich.

I left the internet café about an hour later with that uncomfortable sensation of having wasted time and money. I'd figured out how to basically use the internet and look things up.
After I'd asked the girl working there how I might be able to set up a website and she just shrugged apologetically I made a mental note to ask Miles, Cam or Greg how they suggested I proceed and typed "how to build up a website" and "how do I make my own website?".
I got a bits and pieces of information but not the sort that was comprehensible for

someone who'd just used the internet for the first time.

I passed the book shop and the boutique I never even bothered throwing a glimpse into. I slowed down to briefly read the message on a soggy "Missing" poster of a boy.

Gosh, I hoped they'd find him. Apparently he'd been missing since Tuesday.

I passed the local chip-shop where I jumped into the entrance in a panic, just about knocking over an elderly man who just in time managed to hold onto his fish supper.

"Watch where you're going, Lassie!"

I breathed deeply to calm myself, maybe I'd just imagined it.

I lurked around the corner and sure enough, there were Cam and Al standing at the entrance of the new Indian restaurant across the street, talking and smiling sheepishly, not looking directly at each other, like teenagers. Maybe they'd just bumped into each other while Cam waited for her date. Yes, that would be it. Silly me, all in a panic for nothing! Al wasn't Cam's type and she wasn't his.

I was about to emerge and make my way to the supermarket when Cam looked at her watch, hooked her arm into Al's and they went into the restaurant together, Cam looking fabulous in her dark blue, glittery blouse and pumps.

I felt numb. It wasn't the usual kind of numbness that was just there with lack of sleep and healthy food and the fear of an uncertain future, it was the kind that eventuated to save you from having to suffer pain. Like the adrenalin that kicked in after tripping or bashing your head on something.

I didn't leave the chip-shop. I went inside and stood in the queue for about five minutes, I didn't really notice how long, ordered a fish supper with lots of vinegar and brown sauce and a white pudding, not caring that I could have lived a week from what it cost.

Then I went into the supermarket, went past the bread and the cheese and dairy counter and left with two bottles of cheap wine and one of bourbon and went home.

I woke up fully clothed on the couch the next day to the sound of morning news, the smell of cold grease and sweat and booze… and a bad head-ache.

"Fuck." I croaked to myself as I sat up and brushed the crumbs from my shirt. I had a horrible taste in my mouth and felt dizzy. I looked at the clock and nearly choked when

I saw it was ten past nine. I realized still slightly drunk and a minging, sticky mess. When I searched my mind trying to remember what could be the reason for me feeling like shit and lying on the sofa with two empty wine bottles and a half eaten white pudding next to my head, it suddenly hit me and the numbness kicked in just in time. I got up and dragged myself the bathroom where I got myself cleaned up as well as possible, my head still spinning. How I longed to stay at home. To go to bed and stay there forever.

I couldn't even ring Miles to tell him to please go and open the studio! What if a customer or the deliverer-guy was waiting!

I had to go to work. Even though I felt disgusting and was hung-over, I knew I couldn't possibly survive the day moping around in my vest and knickers watching the news and probably getting pissed all over again. And the state my business in as it was didn't make it any easier either.

I threw on some clean clothes, skipped breakfast and left the flat with my hair still damp. I lit a cigarette and walked briskly. It was starting to get cold in the mornings.

Miles had done a nice job on the entrance so far, maybe he'd be able to finish it when he arrived later on. I silently prayed for him to show up a bit earlier today, knowing this was unlikely to happen.

I made myself a coffee, then checked if there were any appointments due or orders that had to be made, did a bit of tidying up and cleaned my lenses, anything to distract myself, not daring to just stand and look out the window for more than a second.

I heard the door open round about ten and looked up, expecting either Miles or a customer. But it was Cam.

I stared at her for a moment, wondering whether or not I should just hold my breath and pass out. It didn't work. To be hold one's breath that long seemed to require a certain state of calmness. And I wasn't calm. What was I though?

Hurt? Angry? Betrayed? Humiliated?

I didn't really know.

I was numb und hung over and craving a bottle of something strong.

"Hi, Love." She said, seemingly mildly irritated by my sloppy appearance.

I opened my mouth a few times before whispering a "hi".

"Are you alright Lynne? What's the matter?"

She came a few steps towards me and I instinctively backed away, not wanting her to smell yesterday's drink on my breath.

Miles, Love, please come now for God's sake, I begged silently as I frantically looked from left to right to find something to do with my hands.

"Yes, yes. Brilliant. Just slept in so I'm a bloody mess! Haha!"

She didn't laugh along or tut or shake her head saying "silly you", she just came after me, examining my eyes that refused to find her's. "Have you been doing drugs or something, Sweetheart?" Probably too much rambling...

"No, pff!" Not drugs, not really, not marijuana or coke or anything. No lies here to nitpick at, move on!

She came closer and pulled a face.

"You've been drinking!"

"I-"

"Lynne! For God's sake!"

"Hello ladies."

Miles, thank God. Or, the way he was examining me in an oddly Cam-ish way, maybe not.

"You ok there?" There was that fine worry line between his brows.

"Yes, yes. The doorframe look's great, if the weather is alright later I'll grab a paintbrush and we'll keep going."

I dismissed myself and left the room. I was thankful to my bladder at that moment for announcing that I please might want to empty it. At least it had stopped me standing there, frozen, laughing like a bloody moron.

Shit, how the hell was I supposed to react? I didn't even know how to feel.

I washed my face with cold water, took a painkiller for my headache and reemerged from the small bathroom. Cam had sat down in her usual seat and was talking to Miles in a serious tone.

"So she had a drink. She's having a crappy time, leave the girl alone."

"You don't understand, Miles. It's not that she has one or two glasses for comfort here and there, she drinks until she bloody well passes out. She's a terrible alcoholic!"

"Oh fuck, I didn't know…"

I noticed that Cam sounded tearful and couldn't make myself enter the room, knew I couldn't find the words to express…anything, so I stayed behind the doorframe, let myself slide down and buried my face in my hands with shame and agony.

"She was dry, Miles. She was dry for months and months even though she was going through hell. What made her snap?"

"I saw you!" I whispered at first.

They fell silent and I heard Cam get up. "Lynne?"

"I saw you!" it was still a croak but louder this time. My face burned and my hands were shaking. Why was the numbness that had helped me through so much leaving me?

"Sweetheart, are you alright?"

They both peered around the corner into the small hallway I was sitting in nervously.

"I saw you, Cam! I saw you and Al! Yesterday! At the Indian place!"

"Oh God. Oh Lynne." She knelt down and gingerly placed her hand on my shoulder. I didn't have the energy to shrug it away.

Miles, poor Miles didn't seem to know what was going on but stayed leaned against the wall, the worry line between his brows painfully deep with concern.

"Come on, Love. Get up and have a seat and we'll talk about it. You don't want someone to come in and see-"

"Why didn't you tell me, Cam? Why?" I felt so childish.

I wasn't crying. I was calm. But everything inside me was on fire. I couldn't get up.

"I meant to, I really, really meant to. I was worried, with your financial situation and-"

"Please go."

What? Did I really want her to go?

Yes, right now I bloody well did.

"Really? We could-"

"Please, Cam. Please go."

She remained in her crouched position for a few more seconds, perhaps hoping that I'd change my mind. Never had I sent her away before, or shouted at her, or resented or cried because of her.

"Come on, Cam." That was Miles. "I can see your bum crack, Hen. Let me help you up."

She reluctantly removed her hand from my shoulder.

"Alright, Love."

Miles helped her up and she pulled her blouse into position.

"Take care. Please."

She sniffed delicately. She was crying silenty. My Cam was crying. But I couldn't look at her, couldn't face her.

"Please look after her." I heard her whisper to Miles before she left the shop. I assumed he'd nodded.

The next thing I heard was a wail or despair emerging from somewhere deep within me.

A sound I hadn't heard, a feeling I hadn't experienced in a while, resilient as I usually was because I had to be.

I felt Miles next to me, his arm round me, the calming vibration his "ssssh" was sending through his body.

"It's alright. Whatever it is, it'll be alright."

The door opened. "Hello?"

I hastily wiped my eyes and made to jump up, but Miles was faster. "I'll get it, you stay."

I got up slowly and went to the kitchen. I needed caffeine. Badly.

I stood and sipped my coffee, feeling sick, and Miles entered the small kitchen. "Was just a guy collecting something for his wife. It's fine."

I nodded absent-mindedly and we stood in silence.

"So this Al."

He asked carefully, watching my face for a sign hinting that he'd better shut up. I admired the way he dealt with people at his young age.

"Was he someone you dated at some point? Or…" he waited for a reply he seemed to know might never come.

"My boyfriend." I said plainly, my voice still hoarse from tears and drink. "Ex-boyfriend."

He nodded in comprehension.

"Still like him quite a lot, eh?"

I nodded to prevent the tears from falling that were once more welling in my eyes. Where the heck was all the liquid coming from?

More silence as Miles looked for a mug and filled it with still-warm coffee, sugar and long-life milk.

"What happened then?"

I didn't care right then, the numbness had gone, I'd have to grow up and face the facts.

"We were young when we met, really young like, sixteen. He was lovely. He is lovely. Gentle. Nice. Stuff happened. I got involved with alcohol, he got involved with drugs. Not like meth and ecstasy, *"only"* painkillers and stuff but still." I hesitated to have a sip of coffee.

"We fought. A lot. Split up about two years ago."

I exhaled audibly and took another sip, the sick-feeling slowly disappearing as I spoke. It felt sort of good to get it all out.

"I never stopped loving him. Never will, I don't think."

I got a tissue and cleaned myself up. I knew I must still be a blotchy mess. "I fucked up big time. We both. He's moved on, so." End of story.

"Aw Lynne." He gathered me into a hug. I just stood there, stunned, for a few seconds before I relaxed and put my arms round his broad torso. He was warm and felt nice against me. I didn't get a lot of hugs. I didn't want them, mind. But it felt alright.

"It's fine."

"You smell of booze."

"I know."

"You going to stop again before it becomes a problem?"

"Maybe."

"Lynne?"

"Yes, fine. Probably."

He didn't probe any further. He let me go and downed half of his coffee. "Now, you go home, or go to a friend's, or your parents'. I'll take care of this."

"You're not able to-"

"We've not got appointments for anything big today, anything that comes in spontaneously I can manage. You're not well."

After tossing and turning on my sofa watching rubbish on free TV for two hours desperately fighting the urge to bawl, even more desperately fighting the urge not to go for another bottle of crap wine, I finally got up and showered, threw on a fresh change of comfortable yet not-too-sloppy clothes and got the bus to a place I hadn't been for a while. To see people I hadn't spoken to – apart from a few short phone-calls – in a while. Why? I didn't know. Maybe I couldn't have dealt with the pitiful hugs and "there there, Lynni"'s. Maybe I

still held a grudge. Against them. Against myself. Who cared, I needed them now.
Needed love, needed a pitiful hug and a "there there, Lynni" and a mug of cocoa.

I hesitated when I reached the door. Should I go back? Give into the need of alcohol and go home to bawl on my stinky sofa?
And before I could change my mind and do just that, I rang. And waited.
Maybe they weren't in. They were still working, after all. But, I remembered, it was the school holidays.
The door opened and I looked into that kind, warm face. "Lynni," he said with pleasant surprise. "What brings you here after such a long time?"
I smiled shyly and walked into his arms. "Sorry, Greg."

"It's fine, it's fine." He said soothingly as he patted my head. "You've had a lot on your mind lately, we know that. Come inside for a drink."

I was grateful that he turned round to walk inside just then, it gave me time to blink away the tears stinging in the corners of my eyes.

"Phoebe!" he shouted into the kitchen. "Look who's here for a visit!"

There was the stinging again. What the hell was wrong with me? I was usually great at keeping emotions nicely bottled up and shrugging things off! Was I having a nervous break down again? I hoped not.

"Oh, Lynne!" she put aside the tea-cloth she'd been drying a mug with and came over to hug me. Not only did I allow hugs with Greg and Phoebe, I realized once more they felt good and comforting. Also, they were nice enough not to comment on the smell of wine on my breath as a greeting.

I also realized the only grudge I still seemed to hold was one against myself.

Some small part within me seemed to have grown up. Just a tiny bit.

We talked for hours. I was a bit quiet at first, I'd always been shy around Greg and Phoebe, but then I told them all about what had been going on in my life for the past year. ("Hence the recommenced drinking-habit." Greg said, and then added "it's fine, Lynni. We'll get you back to your old self.")

And they in return they told me about theirs. I got my hot cocoa and Greg showed me some beautiful holiday photos he'd taken with his new panorama lens.

We had dinner together and I stayed in their guestroom, which had been mine for a short time and then Georgina's – Mrs. Harris' – before she'd passed away about five years previously.

I lay there and thought, and cried a bit, then went downstairs for another cocoa, then sat on the sofa and thought and cried some more before returning to bed and falling into a very deep sleep.

I awoke at 11:32 in the morning. I'd slept in for the second time in a row. Shit!

All the calmness and comfort was gone from my system immediately and was replaced with the sensation of adrenalin shooting through my limbs. I put my jumper on back to front and ran downstairs. Phoebe was in the kitchen and Greg was sitting at the dining table, apparently correcting some of his pupils' homework.

"Good morning and thanks for everything! Have to go to work!" I shouted over my shoulder as I ran past the living room, just about breaking my legs in the act.

"Slow down, Lynni, I'll drive you over."

Phoebe gave me a quick hug good-bye ("You know you're always welcome, Dear.") and Greg, calm as ever, folded up his reading specs and followed me into the hall where I was now desperately trying to get my arms into the right sleeves of my jacket.

Though I usually preferred to get everywhere on my own account I thankfully accepted Greg's offer and we went outside.

"Working on Sunday's as well now?" he asked me once we'd driven off.

"Have to, it means a few customers more at least and we get the pictures finished faster this way."

"Sorry, if we'd known that we'd have gotten you up."

"That's alright."

After we'd sat in silence for a few minutes I turned my head towards Greg. "Thanks so much, really. I was properly horrid back then for leaving but you're still so good to me whenever we see each other."

He smiled his kind smile and shrugged. More lines had appeared around his eyes since I'd last seen him and his hair was now almost evenly grey.

"It was a messy situation. We're just glad you're mostly alright." He looked at me briefly and winked. Then his face turned more sincere. "But Lynni, don't let the wine become a substantial part of that life of yours again, eh? We don't want you back there."

I nodded.

I jumped out of the car and into the studio so fast I didn't realize it hadn't had to be unlocked and I felt my body relax so suddenly I felt like I might faint. Mile's was standing at a shelf, rearranging our selection of photo albums. He turned around and smiled. "Alright there, Sunshine?" I guessed I looked nothing like a Sunshine and more like a mugging-victim. But I nodded. "Since when've you been here?"

"Since opening time. Made a few calls and managed to swap shifts at Bigg's. Thought you might need another long lie."

"Thanks. I did."

"Get a mobile! Seriously!"

"I know, I know. Coffee."

"Just made some, it'll still be warm. And," he added, rummaging in his rucksack. "I thought you could do with one of these." He produced a greasy looking paper bag with the logo of the bakery two streets away and threw it for me to catch. It contained a huge chocolate croissant.

Oh God, he was lovely, how was I supposed to tell him?

I mouthed a "thank you" and took a bite.

He got me a cup of coffee and gestured for me to sit down and have breakfast. "No set appointments today. You have that and I'm going to get some painting done."

I nodded and continued munching my pastry while wracking my brains. Miles was lovely, and he was my friend, and, I realized, he was probably one of the only people who even tried to get me. And who got me to slow down and have a coffee and a croissant without me verbally biting their head off. One of the few people I cared about. How was I supposed to do this without my heart breaking? Even more, as far as that was even possible?

"Look, we need to talk." It was out before I could do anything about it. It was too painful to postpone it any further. I'd known it was unavoidable for weeks but couldn't face the truth. Familiar situation…

"You breaking up with me?" he said from outside.

I couldn't help but smile a bit.

"Yes. Now come inside."

He did as he was told and pulled a chair up in front of me. "I've sort got something to say too. But you go first, then."

I avoided looking at him and fiddled with the bag now containing a half eaten croissant.

"You know it's been quite difficult financially for me. And I've been having to cut your wages again and again and…Miles, you do a bloody great job here, and you've been a great employee and a better mate…"

I spoke slowly. This lovely man deserved proper, genuine words, not a stammery pile of shite.

"Lynne, say no more. It's fine."

"I'm so sorry."

He nodded and we sat in silence.

"Can we still be friends?" he asked me and I caught a mischievous twinkle in his eyes and got the joke.

"Definitely. Now what were you going to say?"

"Well," he got up and rummaged in his bag yet again and this time produced a messily opened envelope.

"What's this?"

"I thought about what you said, me being young and basically doing not very much. So

I'm going to make something of my semi-awesome grades and go to college."

My eyes widened and for once I looked directly at him. "Really?"

He nodded. "So I started informing myself a bit and applying and was a bit late mind, but I'm going to start training to be a nurse next month. I want to study child psychology sometime later on, I've decided, but better start off like this and build up on the knowledge I'll gain the next few years with a bit of effort."

"That is bloody great, good for you!"

He shrugged modestly. "I wanted to wait a while before I told you I'd have to quit as it's a part time study and I'll be earning money from the practice part of it all and seen as how you're not too well…"

"Oh, but that's great. I'm happy for you."

We sat in silence for about half a minute.

"Do I get to finish that door-project?" he asked more shyly than usual.

"You're more than welcome," I answered and gestured towards the door. Then got up myself. "Right then, you're still getting paid for this month, so get back to work."

"Yes, Sir!"

He was already half outside the door again when he stopped. "You know, I've been meaning to ask you something."

"What?"

"Look, I know you're not all that keen on things like help or pity or people being nice to you in general..." he winked.

"Nope. Go on."

"But technically, if you were to drop your studio flat and move in with my roomy Sam and me...and we'd have split costs and all that...which would really be a big help to me seen as how Sam's thinking about moving in with his boyfriend soon and all…"

He looked at me expectantly. "I wouldn't have to wreck myself and look like I'm in my thirties by next year working at the hospital and at Bigg's – no offence – we – *I* could have proper food! I could take a girl to eat out if we split those electricity costs!"

I tried to maintain a serious expression.

"Think about it." He said, a sly smile on his face, as he went outside to continue his painting.

I did.

Cam, 2015

For once, I had difficulties eating my organic greek yoghurt with oats and sliced banana.

I didn't feel like having a good old, unhealthy bowl of sugary cereal or spoonfuls of chocolate spread either. So I gave up on breakfast altogether, downed my matcha tea and went to the bathroom to apply my face.

After getting lost in thoughts and smudging my eyeliner twice, I gave up on that too and settled for clean teeth and brushed hair. It had been a similar procedure for three days and I was feeling worse rather than better.

I decided I'd let enough time pass and it was time to approach the friend I'd upset so badly.

I called the office and told them I'd be coming later but would stay late if I had to.

Yes, the sketch was almost done. No, I wasn't ill. Or pregnant.

I wondered whether I should wait until Lynne turned up at the studio or go over to her place now and decided on the latter. Then I reconsidered and dialed Miles' mobile number I'd gotten for emergencies of whatever sort. It rang once, twice – "hi?"

"Miles, hi. It's Cam."

"Oh, hiya."

He sounded distracted; I guessed he was on his early shift at the fast food place.

"Is it a bad time?"

"Naw I'm back in the kitchen. Go on."

"I was going to see how Lynne's been."

I closed my eyes and pleaded silently for good news.

"Ah, she's not been all that well. I've been doing a lot of the work here, which was fine. She was in no state to be running a lemonade stand, never mind this place."

Oh f...

"Spent some time at her parent's apparently..."

She'd gone to Greg and Phoebe's, that was a start...

"And then came to work and all that but when I went to see her yesterday evening at her place she was curled up on her couch like an abandoned puppy with a bottle of wine half drained and an empty one underneath her cushion. I don't know what to do."

Shit.

"Look, Miles, I don't know how much she's told you – "

"I know about the ex-lover story. She still seems to be crushing on him big time. Poor lass."

I felt horrible. I'd phoned Alan the evening after Lynne had seen us and told him we couldn't go out anymore. And he'd said he thought it was best that way as well, that he wasn't ready (or maybe not properly over Lynne?) and wanted to focus on the new menu and finding new employees.

I liked him, but I hadn't had the right to ask him out in out in the first place and thus my relief had been bigger than my hurt at his reply. I'd just taken a spontaneous liking to him because…because why? I recalled it happening the evening that dick Tom had dumped me and I'd been sitting at Little John's afterwards drinking and feeling like shit… But how had I thought that'd give me the right?...

"Do you think I should talk to her? Explain that it's over, that it was never all that serious?"

"You can try. You've known her since for ever, you can judge how she'll react better than me. But she is pretty, pretty hurt by it all."

I swallowed and when I spoke, my voice cracked painfully. "I know." I whimpered. "We never even *did* anything, you know? Just a bit of going out and having fun and...some kissing."

I heard Miles draw breath in through his teeth, as if contemplating what to say next.

"I don't think that's what matters to her..."

"I know...bye, Miles."

After crying loudly and hating myself for the best part of a minute, very thankful not to have applied that make-up, I pulled myself together and left the flat.

Apparently Lynne was planning on starting early to compensate the time she'd lost the last two days, as she was just appearing at the outside door when I approached the small block of flats she'd lived in for the past few years.

She didn't notice me at first, just briskly made her way up the opposite pavement, looking like the Lynne I'd known for so many years apart from that resigned, vacant look in her eyes I'd hoped I'd never see again.

I took a deep breath and crossed the road. "Lynne! Love!"

She seemed to snap out of her trance and looked in my direction, her expression suddenly a mixture of all sorts of things, joy or pleasant surprise not being one of them.

She stopped, but said nothing. Just looked at me. I couldn't remember her ever having held my gaze that long.

Once I was right in front of her, I didn't know where to put my hands and clasped them so as to not to fiddle frantically while looking for the right words. What right words?

There were none. I was a dick. A right dick.

"Look, let me explain what-"

"You shagged Al, that's what." Lynne said, her gaze as cool as her voice.

"And came to me for bloody fashion tips as well."

Her voice grew louder with every word and she smashed her bag down on the pavement, causing me to jump. Miles had been right, she'd been drinking again last night.

It had been a while since I'd seen her in such a state: on the verge of tears, her usually attractive features fierce with the desperation to keep them in, black lines under her bloodshot eyes, pale, exhausted.

"Now you tell me what the *fuck* I'm supposed to make of that?"

I wanted to start crying again but I didn't. There was no space for self pity in this conversation, not for me.

"Lynne, I didn't, we… it's over. Really. I called him to say it's over and he thought it was better that way. He-"

"We've known each other for seventeen bloody years, we've been friends for – how could you even think that it's alright to pull off such *crap*!"

"I wanted to tell you-"

"But you didn't!"

I hadn't.

"I love him, Cam. I bloody well love him!"

She could no longer hold back her tears and neither could I. This should have been the point where we hug each other and I tell her that everything would be alright. But I knew it wouldn't. For Lynne and me nothing would be alright again.

My selfishness had ruined a bond you'll form once in a lifetime if you're very, very lucky.

"I can't trust you anymore. Not right now."

She sobbed while trying desperately to find a tissue and ended up wiping her eyes and nose on the sleeve of her jacket.

"I know. I'm sorry."

She nodded in my direction, tears still pouring from her eyes, and walked away.

Lynne, 2015

I'd given up trying to dry my eyes. Once more, I was weeping hopelessly, catching glimpses of people's looks of pity or dismay as I walked to my come down little studio that I loved so much but knew – deep down – I had to let go.

I couldn't possible turn up like this. But I had to. I had an appointment for pregnancy photo-shoot in about half an hour and had to get everything prepared and now that Miles wasn't coming in anymore…I let out another audible sob, then got out my packet of cigarettes and lit my last one. I had to pull myself together.

I felt like the fragile net that had just been holding everything together was finally tearing, causing my world to crumble. I felt like I'd lost everything. Al. Cam. Miles. Shop.

My flat soon too, most likely...I was late in paying rent again, as I often was due to my fluctuating income.

I thought about Miles' offer once more and came to the conclusion it might- just might – be time to get off my high horse and that I'd give him a call before closing later on. I felt so strange after having declined everybody's help for so long but also that I might, just might be on the verge of a nervous breakdown and simply couldn't maintain this way of life.

Before I approached the entrance of the studio, I went into the small niche between the two buildings to throw my empty cigarette packet into the bin and just about had a heart attack.

There was someone sitting there, huddled against the wall, his head rested on his chest.

Every other month or so a homeless person would find this little niche and make themselves comfortable for a while, but usually they had something with them, a sleeping bag or a pile of odd jackets and duvets to keep themselves warm.

I opened the lid and threw the packet away quietly, so as to not wake the man up (a small part of my subconscious was afraid I'd be asked for money when I simply had none to give away) and made to turn around, but a last glance at the sleeping person's face made me linger for another moment. This was no grown man sitting there, half frozen. It was a pale looking boy of maybe fifteen or sixteen with a very thin jacket wrapped around his skinny physique.

His hair was greasy, like it hadn't been washed for over a week, and there were dark rings around his eyes suggesting lack of sleep or illness.

I took a step towards him and realized that his face looked oddly familiar. Where had I seen it before?

Should I approach him? Call the police? Had he been out here all night? All week?

I decided to go inside and think about what I should do or whether I should just leave him be, but at that moment his eyes snapped open and he looked at me in shock.

He scrambled to his feet, his come down rucksack slipping off his lap, and looked in every direction frantically, as if trying to find somewhere to run.

"It's alright" I put my hands up, as if to show I had no mobile or anything I was about to use against him. "It's alright."

"Don't call the police, please. I've…I've got it all worked out, really." He didn't seem as shocked anymore, but he was just about hyperventilating, jumping from one for to another as if calculating whether or not there was enough space for him to squeeze past me quickly without me grabbing him.

"I'm not calling anyone. I'll just…go, if you want, right now."

His features relaxed and he breathed steadily as if trying to calm himself.

He nodded. I nodded in reply, turned to leave and went up the two steps leading to the entrance of the studio.

"Ma'am?" a now shy, quiet voice came from behind me.

"Can I – I mean – do you live here?"

"I work here…"

"Is there a loo?"

His pale face went slightly pink and he looked up at me with, big, tired hazel eyes underneath his messy mop of dark hair.

The boy from the poster.

I took him inside and let him use the toilet, then boiled water for him to have a cup of tea.

He took a sip of it to be polite and then made his way to the door. "Thank you."

I was going to let him go. I had enough to worry about without some kid. But a sudden memory, a flashback, caused me to react. "Wait."

"I'm fine." he said firmly and opened the door.

"No, really, please wait."

"What?"

It may have sounded rude to other's but, even though I wasn't good at reading between the lines, I knew this kid was scared out of his wits about something and had no idea what to do about it.

"What's your name?"

He considered for a moment, his hand still resting on the doorknob. "Peter."

"Liar."

He sighed. "Fine. Ben. My name's Ben."

"And I'm Lynne."

I picked up the cup of tea he'd placed on the small coffee-table and carried it over to him. "Finish this, you look like a bloody popsicle."

The shadow of a smile flashed across his face.

"…and when my adoptive mum died of cancer eight years ago my adoptive dad

couldn't cope anymore. I don't resent him I suppose. He was really, really not well."
Ben sighed once more and looked into his empty cup, his eyes vacant.
"Do you want another one?"
"No thanks."
We sat in silence for a minute. "So that's why you landed in the home again."
He shook his head. "Not again. I was given up for adoption, like, the second I was born. My parents – my adoptive parents – never told me about my real ones. Just that my mum was really, really young and stuff."
I nodded in comprehension, my heart stinging inside my chest.
"Do you resent her?"
He shrugged, keeping an unnaturally straight face, and suddenly found a rack of postcards very interesting. "Did you take these?"

I knew he was trying to change the subject and didn't probe that of his mum and his adoptive parents any further. "Yep."

He took one out. A welsh landscape in black and white. Wild and beautiful. Another painful sting tore through my upper body.

"It's pretty good."

"Thanks."

He sighed heavily and looked at the floor, still fiddling with the postcard. "What do you think I should do?"

I thought for a minute, resisting the strong temptation to get a coffee (I was worried I'd return to find he'd left).

"I was a foster kid."

He looked up at me with genuine interest. "Really?"

I nodded.

"I went into care when I was five. Was in and out of homes."

It had been a while I'd talked about this to anyone but it was easier this time. I felt like this kid, Ben, might understand me.

"And when I was about your age I ran away."

"For how long?"

"A few days, like you."

"Why?"

"Got into some trouble. Doesn't matter."

He didn't ask what kind of trouble exactly, which I was very thankful for.

"And you? Why did you run away?"

He blushed once more. "Was bullied."

"By who?"

"The other foster kids…"

"What for?"

"Don't know, all sorts of stuff. Everything."

"Fuckfaces."

He smiled properly now. "Yeah."

I smiled back. "You know you've got to go back though, right?"

His smile faded and he looked at the floor once more. "I know."

Before I knew what I was doing, I added "come to visit me?"

He looked up at me questioningly.

"If you want."

He nodded enthusiastically. "Yes, please."

"We can have cups of tea and chat. I'd invite you to the pictures or something but…not got a lot of money at the moment."

"Oh, tea's fine, really." He said hastily, as if to prove that he needed no such thing.

"So it's a date."

"I guess."

I realized it had sounded creepy. "You know, not a date-date. Because I'm tiwce your age and shit."

He smiled at me, slightly irritated (I wasn't sure whether about the statement in general or the badass slang). "Yeah?"

"Sorry, kid. No chance."

He got up and stood there, shoulders hanging. "I guess I'll just…go back then."

"That would be good."

He lifted his hand and made a sort of awkward waving gesture, then went to the door. I had one of my sharp-witted moments just then. Chances were, he'd do no such thing. He'd run off and hide somewhere else until he starved or froze to death. "Wait a couple of hours and I'll take you."

"Yeah?"

I nodded. "Yeah, just sit here, read a magazine or…Bobby the Busy Bunny or whatever…"

He raised his eyebrows at the children's books and women's magazines with things like "lose five pounds in one week" and "trend-hairstyles 2016" all over the covers.
"Alright..."

Luckily, Miles came by about two hours later. I'd just completed the photo-shooting with the pregnant woman (she was due in about a week and wanted a "before and after" session) and was tidying up.
"So?" he looked at me expectantly.
"Thought about my offer? Sorry- my request?" he winked.
"I have...I've decided I'd love to help you out by moving in. It would be a laugh, don't you think?"
He pounded the air triumphantly. "Great!"

He noticed Ben slouched in the seat, skimming through an out of date photography magazine.

He held out his hand. "Hi there. Miles. Former employee."

"Hi. Ben. Just...here...at the moment."

A look of recognition passed across Miles' face. He must have seen the posters too and his missing had been on the news.

"Here to have pass photos taken?"

He shook his head and looked at me for help.

"He's a friend of mine." I said quickly. "Here for a visit."

Ben looked at Miles and nodded as if to confirm my statement.

"Oh, alright." Miles accepted this information faster than I'd thought.

He sat down in the chair beside Ben and started to chat.

That afternoon, after Miles had left for his late shift at Bigg's and had made me promise I'd start moving in tomorrow after work, I closed the studio and Ben and I got on the bus that would take us to the street where he lived.

We didn't talk much during the ten minutes that passed. He told me about his school and his grades, I told him about my time there.

I stayed by his side as he explained to the two fosterers and a middle-aged woman who appeared to be his social worker what had happened and why, his face changing colour in a worrying frequency.

Anger and disappointment and then relief passed across the other adults' face during his stammered explanation and apology, then the man left to inform the police that Ben had returned and his foster-mother,

Ann, thanked me for helping and then sent Ben to the bathroom to have a shower, pushing him ahead of herself, obviously trying not to inhale too deeply.

I returned to the bus stop nearby and got onto the next one, put my face in my hands and cried silently. Cried for Cam, for Al, for Ben. Cried because I resented, *hated* myself for the decisions I had and hadn't made in the past.

I went home and took a few swigs of the scotch I'd bought and half finished the evening previously to my own dismay, then threw the bottle away and started packing the few things I owned (how thankful I was at that moment for being a minimalist).

"Hi, Mate!" Miles said, beaming, when he opened the door and saw me standing there with an armful of things.

"There's some more things downstairs. The rest's still at home." I told him, my voice muffled by the pile of items in I was holding. "Take that inside, I'll get the rest."

"Can I use your phone?"

"*Our* phone? Sure!" he said and then leapt down the two flights of stairs, still beaming as he did so. He seemed as excited as an eight year old who's friend's coming to stay over!

I'd just finished the phone call to my landlord to tell him I was moving out when a gorgeous man about my age emerged from what appeared to be the kitchen. "Ah, you must be Lynne! The woman who's taking my place as Miles' roomy!" He said in a lovely Irish accent and scooped me up into a hug.

"Yup, that's me." I confirmed while patting his back awkwardly.

"It's been a great time, Miles is a lovely guy. But, you know, got to move on. I've been with Patrick three years now and we both thought it was time."

I smiled and nodded my approval.

"So, you're the photographer-girl, the one Miles worked for?"

"That's me." I wished I could say something more intelligent…

"Well, good for you. I wouldn't have the nerve to manage a business myself and all that…too dependent." He shook his head as though he regretted this character trait of his.

I grasped my chance to make a statement worth while. "What do you do?"

"I'm a lawyer. Just finished my studies about half a year back. Sure, there are nicer things to do but we've got a reasonable fixed income." He shrugged. "It's also what

Dad does and I never really knew what to do so I decided I'd just follow his footsteps." He shrugged again. He seemed to underline most of his statements with this gesture. "Haven't spoken very much ever since Patrick's been around. Shame really."

"And your Mum? Is she alright with it?"

"Oh yes, she's fine with it. I go round there every other weekend to see her and her new guy's a sport."

Miles returned, huffing and puffing. "Oh, don't worry, Guys. I'm fine." He choked while dumping my three rather heavy boxes beside the front door.

"Well now you know how I felt lugging them to the bus stop and then here, Love."

His boyish grin hadn't faded. "I see you and Sam here have already introduced yourselves?"

"We sure have!" Sam answered and gave me a one armed squeeze. "We're already BFFs."

"That's great, because until you leave for good it's going to be a bit tight..." Miles scratched the back of his head and looked around the small living room as if trying to work out our future sleeping arrangements. "That is if you were planning on moving yourself here straight away, Lynne."

Was I? It would be tight, I decided, as I scanned the living room with three door leading to separate rooms. "If it makes things easier I'm fine staying at mine-"

"Oh no you don't, Roomy!" Miles cut me off. I'll sleep on the couch. Oh don't worry, it's ultra comfy! Just don't get a fright if you hear Sammy or me coming into your room at night."

I felt my eyes widen with dismay and I opened my mouth to tell him he was a pig, but he laughed. "We might need to go through to get to the bathroom. Excuse me for being human!"

"Oh no, it's fine, it's-"

"Just messing with you. Now, how about tea…"

I couldn't help but smile. Me being a nervous wreck lately seemed to be giving Miles the chance to get me back for all the mild bullying he'd had endure during his employment at my studio.

My studio…

"Can I use your computer?" It was time to move forward…

"Yeah, sure."

He gestured towards his rather out of date but seemingly still intact laptop on the coffee table, then went into the kitchen, where Sam was apparently trying to find something edible for the three of us.

After sharing two deep-frozen pizzas, we sat and had a cigarette and the two guys showed me how I might want to set up a website for the studio. I ended up frazzled because I had no idea what either of them was trying to say, and they were frustrated because I was a silly whiney git, so I let them do most of it, throwing in an idea here and there. In the middle of the process, Sam's mobile rang and he left the room to discuss his future living arrangements with Patrick.

"Got you camera with you?" Miles asked after a while, his brows furrowed in concentration.

"Still at mine. Why?"

"Because you might want to put some pictures up on the site, you know, to give people an idea of what your work looks like."

That did sound reasonable.

"Alright, then…" with a final click and a triumphant "ha!" he turned his laptop towards be and waited for my reaction. "What do you think?"

I studied it silently for a few minutes. Te design was simple yet attractive. All the necessary information was there. Even to me it looked easy to operate. I liked it. I *loved* it. "Thanks Miles. And Sam. I really needed the help." I felt myself blush as I realized what I'd just said. *You're Lynne bloody Wilson, for God's sake! What are you doing, begging people for help?* An angry voice said at the back of my mind.

It's fine. You're just fine, Love. Another, much stronger voice now said and I relaxed. I looked at Miles, who had been following my inner battle the last few seconds and quickly averted my eyes, but he just winked and ruffled my hair. "Yuck, stop that."

He laughed heartily. "That's my Lynne."

He closed his laptop, then suddenly looked a tad more serious. "I know it's not a very good subject at the moment...you spoken to your pal Cam at all?"

I choked on the sip of coke I'd just been swallowing.

"Sorry, we don't have to-"

"It's fine. I'm just being a big baby."

"Alright, what happened then?"

I told him about Cam coming to my block of flats, apologizing and crying. About me not being able to, or rather not finding the strength to forgive her.

I sighed once I'd finished and pretended to examine my nails critically for a moment while Miles spoke. "I get it, you know. I get that you feel hurt, betrayed and all that."

I swallowed and nodded briefly, avoiding his gaze.

"But I do think you should try to forgive her. We all make mistakes, stupid decisions…we're only human. Not one of these…" he pated the surface of his laptop noisily, "where you just type in some combination or other or click at a certain thing and it does exactly what you want. There's a *huge* spectrum of colours in between black and white."

I nodded again, less enthusiastically this time.

"This Al guy… have you thought about having a word with him?"

Had I. Of course I had. But then the memories came flooding in. Especially those of the time everything started to go wrong…when our businesses had started going downhill and I'd caught Al dealing to make some extra money…it had begun when he'd gotten medication for his bad back and had sort of got really badly hooked…a few days after I'd lost a customer for turning up at their house and ranting at them in foul language for not paying their bill (a wedding shoot that was supposed to cost three hundred quid) and kicking the shit out of their car. The police took me home, so wasted on bad wine I could hardly walk. It quickly became a habit and henceforth I'd been in a similar state up to four nights a week.

On a quiet evening, when we'd both been off drugs of any kind, we sat and talked, and had come to the conclusion that we weren't good for each other. It had turned into a devils circle, Al not being able to concentrate on the pub his Dad had left him in charge of over worrying about me, me having the same problem with my business over worrying about Al and his problem. We were both unable to stop.

And so Al had left, and had somehow managed to get back on his feet on his own accounts, and so had I. Until now, that is. Was he still clean? How was his business running?

I couldn't help but wonder.

I realized Miles had been watching me, not wanting to disturb my thoughts. How long had I been sitting here, my mouth hanging open like an idiot?

I fell asleep eventually and awoke the next morning rolled up on the sofa feeling surprisingly relaxed, even content.

Miles gave a grunt of a snore and I realized he'd dozed off beside me sitting in an upright position, his head slouched forward. *That's going to hurt like fuck later*, I thought to myself as I sat up.

"Rise and shine!" came Sam's voice from the kitchen. He must have heard me yawn. I smelled the homely, comforting smell of strong coffee as I approached the kitchen myself. Sam smiled across the room as he emptied a packet of supermarket baps into a bread basket. "Sleep well?" I nodded while I looked around the small but astonishingly tidy kitchen for a cup or mug of some sort and, as if he'd read my thoughts, was handed one by Sam.

"Thanks."

"Get yourself a coffee, I'm just going to pop these on the coffee table with some chocolate spread and jam. Come through when you're ready."

I filled my mug with coffee and took a minute to lean against the worktop and close my eyes. I was confused. Felt hurt and upset but also had a strong sensation of gratitude and excitement. Maybe I'd had to hit rock bottom (I hoped that this was as far as it would go at least) to enable things – including myself – to get better.

Sam's boyfriend came in just as we were finishing breakfast, had a cup of tea and started to help Sam sort out his things. He was just as lovely as Sam, a bit quieter perhaps.

After I'd got washed and dressed and with the three men bustling about (I'd offered my help but the place was too small for the three of them let alone four of us to be raking about) I sat on the sofa and put on Miles's laptop in the hope of having an E-Mail or two about a job. I was a bit disappointed to find no one had written. Then again, I recalled, the website was mere eighteen hours old. I'd have to give it time.

I thanked Miles and Sam and wished latter all the best for his future, then left for work. It was a quiet day. Not just because there weren't many people in, but because I felt Miles's absence like a physical pain. Of course I was used to being alone with myself and my thought for hours on end at home, but at work I'd always been able to look forward to a pleasant chat and a fag or even the presence of another human being.

The thought of coming home to a friend to have a meal and watch TV with later on cheered me up immensely and thus I had the energy to finish the painting of the doorframe, clean the whole place from top to bottom, including the inside of the coffee machine and get the pictures from the pregnancy shoot developed.

I knew I was scrubbing and polishing madly because I was trying to block a whole lot of things out, but it was fine as long as it was working and preventing me from sneaking a bottle of scotch later on. That would be hard in future. Another good thing about having a roommate.

About an hour before closing time, I heard the door open and a pale, familiar looking figure stepped inside.

"Didn't expect to see you back here this quick."

Ben smiled shyly and shrugged, dropping his rather crappy looking schoolbag on a chair.

"School's out and I thought I'd say hi." He said in a slightly too defensive tone of voice.

"That's nice. Tea?"

"Yes, please."

I returned a minute later with a mug of sweet tea for Ben and a coffee for myself to find him gingerly turning the stand with my postcards, looking at them admiringly, as he had last time.

"I was going to ask you something."

"You're a bit too young for me. But we can still be friends."

He coloured and tutted in an annoyed but still amused way. "No. I mean, I was going to ask you…the thing is, we don't get much pocket money at the home. Not anything really. And I was wondering if you were maybe looking for someone to give you a hand…"

He coloured an even deeper shade of crimson. "But it's a stupid idea, I know. Sorry."

I looked at him apologetically. "No, it's not. I completely get it. And I appreciate it and would love a hand and a bit of company around here. It's just that I've just had to let my friend Miles, who worked here, go, because I've just not got enough income at the moment."

"Oh, alright." He tried to cover up his disappointment by shrugging and flipping through a magazine. I felt really bad, as I liked the kid even though I hardly knew a thing about him except his first name.

"But you might want to go round the town a bit, into the chippy or the paper shop, they're always looking for someone. Just, you know, tidy yourself up a bit and stuff" I added, pointing awkwardly at his long-ish, slightly greasy hair. He covered it half heartedly with his hand and nodded. "I'll do that. Thanks."

He emptied his mug and picked up his bag. "Thanks for the tea. See ya."

"Wait a minute." I said impulsively, without really knowing why.

"Yeah?"

"Do you want to go to the pictures or something at the weekend? My treat?"

Lovely gesture, Love. With what money again? And is that even appropriate? Or legal??

But I could worry about that later.

He hesitated, obviously surprised about this sudden offer of friendship. "Alright, yes."

"Pick me up at work on Saturday and we'll take the bus over."

"Sounds good." And with that, he left.

Lynne, 1998

My vision was blurry with tears of both cold and anger. A kind of pain I'd not had to encounter very often before. Never had I been so openly and obviously despised as by that Mrs. Harris, who seemed to be treating me with increasing disrespect. She'd mostly avoided trying to have proper conversation with me for the past few weeks since she'd arrived here, but had apparently had a very bad day, according to Phoebe, as she was having "migraine and terrible problems sleeping". Still, to sit at the dinner table and probe a sixteen-year-old girl who had a traumatizing childhood of wandering from one dysfunctional family into another about that past…downright horrid. I hated this self-pity but I couldn't help but feel upset.

I heard the words again and again, running through my head like a broken record.

"...been meeting boys again, have you? You just watch out that that bastard of a girl doesn't end up a tart like her mother. Dishonoring the two of you more than enough as it is walking about like a mess." She'd said to Greg and Phoebe, waving her fork in my direction, particularly at my hair, splattering spaghetti-sauce all over the tablecloth.

Phoebe, sweet as she was, was pathetic when it came to her mother and just wrung her hands anxiously muttering that "Lynne's a lovely girl, Mummy, and if she wants to go out with a boy that's just fine. Isn't it, Love? She *is* sixteen."

"Old enough to leave care and to stop scrounging!"

Greg, sweet as *he* was, knew that Phoebe was putting all her strength into making her horrible mother feel better and simply sat there with clenched teeth and nodded once aggressively before stabbing his plate of spaghetti. He was usually such a calm, patient human being, but he'd grown protective of me, like a Dad should. I loved him for being cross with Mrs. Harris for how she treated me, and also for trying not to show in front of Phoebe, *for* Phoebe. But I so wished that someone would say something more than what "a lovely girl Lynne" was and put her in her place. She felt unwell, yes, well, a lot of people felt unwell as far as I knew and didn't go around treating others like shit.

I'd clumsily excused myself, then gotten up and left the house, unable to be near that woman let alone down a plate of spaghetti in her presence.

But where to go? This was one of these rare moments that being alone wasn't an option. Cam? Cam was away for the weekend to see her Mum's Aunt with her parents. Apart from that, there wasn't really anyone.

After hesitating for a moment or two, I walked a few streets further past the local book, paper and chip shops to Little John's. I hadn't been there since I'd gone out with Al the first time a few weeks previously. Since then we'd only seen each other at school and the one or the other time he'd picked me up at home on a Friday to see a film or just go for a walk and get a poke of chips. He'd not attempted to kiss me again, he'd just gingerly taken my hand in his for a few minutes at a time while sitting in the cinema or on a bench, our finger's greasy

with either popcorn or chip fat. I supposed it was a friendly gesture. I'd seen girl-friends do that. I was thankful that Cam seemed to understand that I wasn't really a hand holdy sort of person and neither did that nor did she follow me to the bathroom (how the hell did girls manage to pee with people standing outside the cabin talking about maths-test-results?) But somehow, for some reason, I wanted to hold Al's hand.
I entered the restaurant, a wave of immediate relaxation flooding through my body from the warmth. In my frustration I'd forgotten any piece of appropriate clothing. There he was, wiping tables. Thank goodness. That would have been bloody awkward, standing here with nothing on me except the odd two pence piece in my jeans pocket.

I wanted to walk over to him. But then I remembered I wasn't one of those cool people that just go over to someone and say "hiya, how're things going?" or something like that. I just stood there, frozen to the spot, and gawped at the screen showing rugby in a far corner until he looked up from wiping tables and came over to me, smiling and saying "table for one?" with a wink.

"Depends, what can I get for...two pence and a yucky old chewing gum wrapper?" There it was again, that easiness that had been there since the first time we'd properly talked. I felt my heart rate increase almost painfully. Yuck.

He laughed. I've got about twenty minutes 'til my shift ends. Sit down here if you like and we'll go for a walk or whatever."

I nodded and sat down at a table for two and looked around. I should ask if I can phone home, I decided, or Greg would be running to the police station within the next half hour.

Al's Dad, Mr. Johnson, kindly let me and I had a very relieved and tearful Phoebe on the other end. "I'm so sorry, Sweetheart, you know how she gets and she's had a really bad day."

"I know. It's fine"

"Where did you say you are?"

"At Little John's. To see Al. My *friend.*" Had I stressed the last word enough? Too much perhaps for it to sound casual? Damn.

"Alright. It's good that you called, we were getting a bit worried."

"Sorry. I'll be home in a few hours, I just need to calm down."

"I understand."

"But I'm not a tart."

"I know, Love."

"Alright, bye."

I'd already made to put the phone down, but heard Phoebe's voice and held it to my ear once more. "What?"

"I was just going to say…you know…you don't think very well of your Mum. I get that. You've had a hard time. But it doesn't make her a bad person because she did these things."

Did it not? I'd never thought about it. All I could seem to see before my inner eye when I thought about my birth mother was a lot of things children shouldn't see or hear. Being hungry and unwashed a lot of the time. Lacking human contact except for the neighbor's two children as she hadn't put me in playschool. A childhood without a father, as he'd most likely been one of her clients. I'd always dreamt up a Dad who had been in love with my mother, who had been sweet and kind and wanted a baby daughter more than anything, but whom my mother had left without telling him she was pregnant or who'd left on his own accounts because she'd repeatedly betrayed him.

But I was old enough to understand what had probably been the case and face this truth, even though it hurt.

But what I also remembered now was never having been hit or pushed, not until I'd lived with the Baxters about three years later, that is. Thank goodness that hadn't lasted long.

Neither did I remember hugs or sitting on her lap or any other form of physical contact, but she'd never risen but a finger against me. I sighed heavily to prevent tearing up. I didn't want to think about that right now.

"I know. Thanks."

"See you later, Lynne."

Al approached me, removing his apron as he did so and wiped his hands dry on it.

"Coming?"

We walked outside and discovered that it was still freezing cold.

And as I still didn't have many layers on, we decided against walking through the park and went to his place.

"We can watch something there if you like or just sit and chat."

We didn't turn on the TV. Al just sat down next to me on the living room sofa and asked me what was wrong.

"Nothing?" I said and shrugged, avoiding his gaze a tad too pointedly. "Why?"

"Fibber. Come on, Mate, what's up. You've never just come by to say hi."

"Well then, I won't next time."

"Of course you will, now talk to me."

I told him all about what had happened, ending my rather passionate speech with "stupid old fart". The kindest of words I could find to describe Mrs. Harris.

Why was I even trying to be a lady? It was just Al, after all.

He didn't say anything, just sat and looked at me for a moment, as though deep in thought.

I wasn't very good at reading people, but I didn't see Al as a person who thought very much. Not that I thought him to be thick. Just that he was one of those people who just did things and took things as they came without overanalyzing. Or something.

I caught myself looking him up and down, taking in his face, his expression, his physique like I'd never done with anyone before.

He smiled and pulled me into a hug. "Don't fret about it. You know better than her who you are and who you aren't, that's all that counts, really."

"But who am I?"

He pulled away just enough to be able to look at me. "You're Lynne. That nice, funny girl that swears like a lorry driver I like to be around." I blushed. Damn, I'd been trying so hard to reduce my use of strong language and bad words to a minimum. A bit. Not really.

"Well…thanks."

He laughed and then, after hesitating he leaned in and kissed me. He pulled away after giving me a short, soft peck to see my reaction, then kissed me again, moving his lips slowly, becoming increasingly passionate. I was irritated, as this was the last thing I'd expected to happen this evening. But that feeling was left lying somewhere at the far corner of my mind, as it was overpowered by a feeling so much stranger and so much stronger.

I was breathing heavily, the world behind my eyelids was spinning with dizziness.

I felt some part of my lower body cramp in a way I'd never felt before as Al let his hands wander over my arms, down to my legs and back up my hips, where they rested and he pulled my body closer to his.

We...well...*did it* that evening. It was fairly silent, a bit clumsy and only hurt a tiny bit. I'd had no idea what to expect as I'd never talked about sex to anyone and had been a bit shy when he'd gingerly slipped a hand under my shirt but, to my own surprise, encouraged this enthusiastically.

We lay there on his bed - to which we'd moved at some point, not wanting to leave the obvious marks of *it* on Mr. and Mrs. Johnson's settee – staring at the roof, not really knowing what to do or say next. This was very awkward, as conversation and even silence had been such an easy thing with Al before.

"So..." I said finally.

"So?"

"I should be going."

And with that, I stumbled out of bed and into my clothes, as did he a few moments later.

"I'll be seeing you at school. Thanks for..." I blushed. Thanks for what? "Talking and stuff."

I made my way towards the door.

"Lynnette?"

My heart jumped when I heard him say my name and I felt tears burning in my eyes. This must have been the fourth time I'd gotten weepy in one day. Damn Mrs. Harris. Damn Alan. "Yes?" I croaked, suppressing a sob. What was *wrong* with me all of a sudden?

"I wasn't…I…I mean, please don't think I was just trying to…"

"I don't. Me neither."

"I like you."

I nodded imperceptibly, then turned around and nodded again as soon as I had my emotions under control.

"Yeah." And then, so as not to be a total git. "I like you too."

Gosh, could it get more soppy?

He walked me home after a long embrace that brought me to the verge of tears once

more and, once we were at the driveway of Greg and Phoebe's, gave me a short, gentle kiss.
So yes, it could.
Only once I'd gone inside, had wished Greg and Phoebe good night (Mrs. Harris was already in bed, thank goodness for that) and was getting into my pajamas did I realize we hadn't used birth control of any kind. But then, it had only been once, what could possibly happen?

A few weeks had passed since "the occurrence", which I'd started to call it in my attempt to not think of it as what it really was. Funny, really, that I was able to talk about "that school lunch being fucking bad" or to Mr. Whatsisname-Alphabully "fuck off you cunt or you'll be in really deep shit", but went scarlet when overhearing

Anna Craigton about having sex with her boyfriends, using the actual terms in her detailed descriptions. And so, I made the decision to henceforth refer to it as "the occurrence" or, when not referring to that specific "occurrence", to use the term coitus or otherwise "it". "Doing it" was a term of such common use for people my age that it was just like using the actual word. No one said coitus. Or just "it". That would do.

But the whole thing turned out to be less complicated than I'd thought. Al and I still met after school now regularly, were perhaps a tad less confident in each other's company than before…"the occurrence", and shared a shy kiss or hand-holding from time to time.

This lack of groping or nakedness or intimacy of any sort was probably due to the fact that neither of us was bold enough to ask the question that lingered between us so heavily you could almost touch it.

"What is this? What do you want? What do I want? What's "acceptable" for the rest of the society? Do we give a fuck about the rest of the society?"

But, as far as I was concerned, things were just fine. As far as I could tell, real, actual relationships ended up in tearful screaming matches and the throwing of things at one another, at sixteen at least.

I came home to the smell of Phoebe's Bolognese. She had piles of it frozen if a quick dinner was needed or she didn't feel like cooking. I loved it, Bolognese was my favourite.

"Hi, Sweetheart." I heard her voice come from the kitchen.

"How was your day?"

I shrugged. "Can I help?" Phoebe smiled and nodded her head. She'd never had a problem with my laconic way of expressing myself, unlike Mrs. Harris, who described it as "rude" and "disrespectful" and took it very personally. "It's nearly ready, go and sit down."

I left the kitchen and sat down at the dining room table. I heard Mrs. Harris' nagging voice, distant at first, then growing increasingly louder as Greg helped her down the stairs "…don't know why you didn't put the bedroom in the bottom floor, when you got this place, you might have thought about me moving in at some point or other…"

"Hiya, Lynni". Greg said, forcing a smile, as he helped hi still-nagging mother-in-law onto the seat opposite mine. "Hi Greg. Hi

Mrs. Harris." Nothing. Then "Why is she not in the kitchen helping my daughter?"

"It's fine, Mummy. She asked if she could help." Phoebe came to my defense while placing a big pot of spaghetti Bolognese onto the middle of the table.

"Come now, Georgina, the girl's probably had a long day."

"Long day, long day. When I was her age, I..."

But what exactly she was or did or said when she was my age I didn't hear, I was too busy clutching my stomach as a wave of nausea came over me.

I must have turned as white as I felt, because Phoebe looked at me worriedly and out her hand on my forehead.

"Everything all right?"

"Fine." I managed to utter through clenched teeth.

Abbie Lambert, the girl I sat next to at school, had been off sick last week with the flu. I'd probably caught that. Or the fish fingers that had been served for lunch had gone bad. Could fish fingers go bad? Didn't ninety percent of them consist of preservatives?

But I didn't get to think about my theory or the idea of starting one of those organic-only diets that was never going to happen, as I felt sick once more and this time felt it would be best to remove myself from the dining table and the pot of spaghetti.

"Lynni?"

"Sweetheart?"

"How utterly rude that girl is!"

But I didn't care how rude I was. I ran to the toilet and threw up noisily until I felt like I had no organs left inside me, then dragged myself outside to sit on the stairs. I hadn't puked for years and had forgotten how utterly horrible it felt.

I realized that Phoebe was kneeling next to me, gently feeling my slightly perspiring forehead, and Greg was standing in the doorframe between living-room and hallway, looking concerned.

"Are you feeling ill? Do you just want to go to bed and stay home tomorrow?"

I nodded, unable to put on a cheerful smile and say "I'll be fine by tomorrow, don't worry! Damn those rotten fish-fingers! Ugh!"

So I clumsily got to my feet and fell onto the couch, which currently doubled as my bed, let Phoebe take my temperature, and tried to go to sleep so I could ignore the remaining sick-feeling. I could hear eating noises and conversation that included a lot of medical, kidney-related terms and the occasional complaint from Mrs. Harris how "that girl is just trying to get out of school! She's just the type!", and eventually fell asleep.

I felt better when I woke up the next day. Phoebe had phoned the headmaster of her school to say she'd be a few hours late and offered to take to see a doctor when I confirmed that I felt better but awfully tired and just not quite myself. She was very cautious about illness and always said things like "better safe than sorry", even though I reassured her it was bound to be the phony fish-fingers.

She probably thought I had an ulcer from post-traumatic stress or something.

Once there, we waited for a while, reading crumpled magazines from last year that held the latest information about why actress "Deirdre O'Connor (37) has been seen without husband Gary (44) repeatedly at all the recent events. Are they getting divorced? Is this young man O'Connor was photographed with her new lover?" and how "this new high intensity yoga workout will help you drop 10 pounds in 10 days" and things like that.

I felt bad about Phoebe missing work because of this. "Go if you like, I'll be fine." She tutted. "Nonsense. I'm not moving an inch 'til you've been in there to see Dr. McDonald." And that was that.

When I was called in twenty minutes later, Phoebe asked carefully if she should come with me, but I decided that – though I was touched as no one had ever asked if they should come in with me even when I was small, it once took a family three weeks to realize I had a really bad bladder infection at seven - at sixteen, this was something I should be able to do by myself.

"Hello Miss..." before he could say my actual surname – I hated to even *hear* it – I said "Baker." He looked up from his screen, his eyes narrowed in incomprehension at first, then seemed to understand and smiled. "Baker, of course. Miss Lynnette Baker. What can I do for you?"

I opened my mouth, then shrugged. In a lot of previous families I'd been in, no one had been marched to the doctor for having a little stomach cramp. What if he laughed? Then he was a dick. That's what.

"I felt a bit sick yesterday."

He didn't laugh, but he smiled. But I didn't think of him as a dick. He seemed fine.

"How much a bit sick?" He winked.

"Well, a bit really sick." I hesitated. "I puked."

"Have something bad to eat?"

"The fish fingers at school were funny."

"Might be a case of food poisoning…how do you feel now?"

"Fine. Tired." I'd felt tired a lot lately. Really, horribly tired and lacking the energy to even go to the loo when doing homework. But right now it was easy enough to explain due to the current hour.

"Diarrhea or constipation?"

"No."

He wrote this down.

"Are you on any medication at all?"

"No."

After feeling my stomach and doing one or two other tests, Dr. McDonald came to the conclusion that I may have something called gastritis. There was no way to know for sure without a gastroscopy, however, a procedure which apparently included being sedated and having a tube with a miniature camera or something stuck on the end inserted into one's stomach through the mouth. I decided against this, got my prescription for acid-binding tablets and my sick line for school and went to the waiting room to collect Phoebe.

Lynne, 2016

It was astonishing how easy it was to sit here in silence with a kid I hardly knew. Usually, being in silence with someone I hadn't known for ages gave me a sensation of suffocating on thick air, which was ironic. As a photographer, I spent a lot of time one on one with people. During this time however, I recalled, I was giving them brief instructions and concentrating on my images. That was different. But Ben and I, I discovered, were completely at ease just sitting here on a bench eating ice cream. I'd have liked to take him to the pictures or something, I'd not been for ages myself, but though my financial situation was more stable than it had been before my new living-arrangement, I still had to watch what I gave money out for.

I'd been getting the odd booking to take pictures at weddings since I got the website about three months back. I was doing fine.

This was the third time I'd met up with Ben. Though there were quite a few years between us, I'd begun to see him as a friend. We'd fallen out a bit on one occasion when I'd asked him about his childhood in an attempt to make smalltalk (something I should stop attempting). He got upset and left the flat. I'd been worried I wasn't going to see him again. But he'd visited me at the shop a day later without commenting on what had occurred. It was better this way as far as I was concerned. No awkward apologies and things like "oh that's all right you were upset". I didn't ask him about his childhood henceforth, and he didn't ask me. We were both foster-kids. We were both messed up. We were doing our best to deal with life. That's all there was to know, wasn't it?

"Lynne?"

"Mh?" I asked back, failing at my attempt to remove a dark blodge on my t-shirt. Why did ice-cream have to be so damn melty...and why did I have to have chocolate?

"I was thinking. I'm seventeen. And nearly done with high school."

"Mh." Where was this going?

"I'd like to go to college. And I'd like to leave care."

"Ok."

"Yeah."

"To study what?"

"Communication and Literature."

I suppressed a snort? "Communication?" I threw his a sideways glance.

"Why not?"

"You're not really…Comminucative."

"I'd like to write. Novels and things. Or journalism, maybe."

I nodded in acknowledgement and we sat in silence for another few seconds while finishing our ice cream.

"Is that all?" I'd had something far worse in mind. In films, when they say "I was thinking", someone is usually about to utter a crazy idea.

"Can I live with you and Miles?"

I choked on my cone.

"Good joke. If you fancy sleeping on the kitchen floor. Because you're not getting the couch, kiddo."

He seemed taken aback, but it was hard to tell.

"No, really. I'll apply for this benefit for care leavers and I want to do a bit of work while studying. We could get a bigger place. The three of us."

"That was a lot of words." I examined my nails while I processed them.

"So?"

I thought about it and he respected my need to take time, though I knew that, had I turned to look at him, he would be gawping at me wide eyed in suspense. Eugh.

"We don't know each other very well." I said slowly. "Yet." I added when I saw the destroyed look in his eyes.

"When I left care and started to work, I moved into a half-way home first." A part of my life I really, really…really didn't feel the need to reminisce.

"But surely you could move in with some other students, you wouldn't have the long train journey to Edinburgh or wherever every day and all that. It'd take you, what, an hour?"

He nodded and averted his eyes, then sighed heavily. "Suppose you're right. It was just a thought."

"I know."

"But," he said and straightened up, enthusiasm returning to his voice and his features.

"say I come to work for *you* during school holidays or in the afternoons?" He looked at me hopefully for the second time and I hated my guts for breaking his vulnerable heart.

"I'm not quite set up properly yet, so…."

He nodded sadly once more. I was a terrible person.

"But I will keep my eyes open for jobs and I insist you visit me. And I'll visit you."

Fuck. How much did a ticket to Edinburgh (or wherever) cost again? Did it pay off to go for one day? If not, could I face sleeping on the couch in a flat that was shared by five teenagers? *Male* teenagers with greasy hair, burping and bringing home girls and laughing about fart-jokes? I needed to stop being so prejudiced.

I nodded firmly when he eyed me sceptically. "I *will*".

Eventually, we parted and both went home.

I realized when I walked past Little John's that my stomach still clenched and I had a lump in my throat. I hadn't seen him again, nor had I spoken to Cam. She'd tried once or twice to contact me but I couldn't, just couldn't, face answering her phone calls. Stupid trust issues.

Lynne, 2016

Days passed. I felt like shit.
Weeks passed. I felt like shit.
Months passed. I felt...ok. A hint of shittyness crept into my emotions now and then on particularly shitty days. But all in all, I was coping. I was still considering having a few therapy sessions and/or some anti-depressants. But I felt like I was slowly – excruciatingly so – but steadily going uphill.
I was fine living with Miles, more comfortable around him than I'd thought, even if he did bring a ladyfriend – usually drunk - home on one occasion or the other. I then mumbled a "hi" and rapidly raised the TV volume significantly.
He was together with this one girl, Anne, for about a fortnight before she broke his heart for one of the cool kids and sent him home

with puffy eyes and the need to watch Disney Movies while shoveling transfats into himself. I'd happily joined in. She'd actually tried to have a conversation. With me. To be fair, we'd been having tea together. Polite conversation or smalltalk seems to play a substantial role in the act of collective ingestion.

She'd wanted to "hook me up" with "one of the guys", an offer I'd politely declined.

A few weeks later, Sam and Pat (I loved. Loved. LOVED them) were there (also for tea, but they'd actually taken us to this semi-ridiculously fancy dancy-spectacular-fifty quid for one tiny pea fermented for three decades and flambéed-sort of place to celebrate their engagement.) and had wanted to "hook me up" with "one of the guys", which I politely declined. Pat had asked me with genuine interest whether I was homosexual or perhaps a-sexual, as I hadn't hit it off with Miles "that sexy piece of hunk" (Sam had earned a very jealous glance from Pat for this statement, but didn't seem to hold grudges).

I'd thought about the a-sexual thing for a minute. No, not entirely.

But I just felt I was done with "guys", or men, or, for that matter, any other person of any gender and/or gender identification in any romantic and or sexual way. Done.

Too much drama, too many tears, too much feeling like shit. And, come to think of it, too many body fluids for my liking.

Gosh, I was an eleven year old stuck in the body of a thirty-two year old female.

Though I hadn't minded *his* body fluids all that much. Gross…

Ben was doing his exams and about to start college in St. Andrews. He'd left the - to him

- purgatorial state that had been his care home and had found a flat in the center of St. Andrews he shared with two other students and was still on the lookout for a job.

We'd kept our promises and he'd come to see me. I was glad he hadn't (yet) wanted to "hook me up" with "one of the guys"…eugh. And work wise…I was coping. I was assignments for weddings, newborn- and pregnancy shootings, birthdays and one or two girls in their twenties wanting sexy underwear photos as one-year anniversary gifts for their boyfriends. And, of course, the regular passport and toddler photos and please-please-buy-one-and-I'll-take-off-25%-picture-frame sales that had kept me above water for over two years. Frantically gulping for oxygen and constantly seeing the light, but nevertheless.

As for Cam…she seemed to have given up on me. And the moment I realized that she hadn't attempted to contact Miles or myself for some time, I felt it was best to let go of each other. I'd felt a pang of sadness. Of loss. Guilt. Regret. Basically, too many feels for one Lynne to cope with yet again.

That could have been my life. Just plodding along existing in this quite satisfactory routine of mine. Get up, have coffee and fag, work, coffee and fag and lunch, meeting Ben, come home, coffee and fag, tea, dry Mile's tears of heartbreak and watch singing cups and saucers yet again while eating ice-cream, (wishing I could, for once, watch my beloved American sitcoms), check E-Mails. And, eventually, the sweet, close to orgasmic pleasure of lying in a cool bed and drifting off to sleep. And all of this almost completely without the urge to guzzle wine until I passed out. I was feeling very dry and very happy with myself. I still loved my caffeine. I'd cut down the nicotine a bit (which was a start). I'd taken to eating rather unhealthy amounts of cookie dough ice-cream, but I came to realize I'm just a human being too.

But it wouldn't be my life if that had been it. Because life – my life, to be specific - was a melodramatic, attention-seeking fairyprincess/bitch.

It all began when there was a frantic ringing at the doorbell (I really didn't have the nerve to let someone into my sheltered quiet life that was possibly being followed by someone armed). Excited as I was, I jumped up and answered. My visitor (as they always did) took his time to prevent him or herself collapsing and finally, Ben came around the corner, grinning.

"Got yourself a ladyfriend?"

"No! Better!"

I was dying to tell him – anyone! – my own brand new oh so beautiful news but decided to let him spill first.

"I got a job! A real job!"

"Good for you. Drink? Juice or coke?"

He nodded.

He followed me into the kitchen where I poured us both a glass of juice. "Where? What?"

I wasn't prepared for what came next. "Little John's. Waiter."

"Oh. There." I smiled forcefully. "Good." It had been me, after all, that had told him about the place. And it didn't mean I had to go by there right now to lick "the owner's" face.

"Yeah." We stood sipping our juice and nodding at our glasses like a pair of idiots until Ben broke the silence. "And you? Found a guy?"

"Better! Ha!"

"A girl?"

"A job!"

He squinted at me, as if trying to figure out whether I was mocking him.

"But you've got a job."

"Duh. Come and read this."

I went to the sofa and opened the E-Mail I'd received earlier that day. Miles was still at work and I was left to let the information and chances it beheld sink in all alone.

His eyes widened as they scanned over the E-Mail. "Wow."

"I know!"

The door opened and Miles came in, tired looking. "Hiya, oh hi mate."

"Hi!"

"I'm starving! Still some of those baps left?"

"I'll get them and we'll have cheese and ham rolls."

While the three of us sat and had tea, I decided an adequate time had passed for me to tell Miles about the job. "I got this Email earlier on."

"Wow, you *do* have friends!"

"Shut up!" I nudged Ben in the side with my elbow, who was sniggering into his roll. That got him to stop. "Ouch! Your elbow's pointy!"

"There's this new fashion magazine, *Nostalgie*, and I got an Email from a chief-editor-slash-designer sort of woman that they'd like to hire me to do a shooting for a summer collection of dresses and things."

He let it sink in while munching away.

"On Crete!" Ben added. "That's Greece!"

"Wow, cool. Good for you!" He nodded in acknowledgement.

I blushed. I could hardly believe it myself. "It's funny though. Because I never sent an application, for all they know, I could be rubbish and my website could be all lies!"

"But to get one of the big guys this Nostalgic thingy's probably not known well enough. They'd be broke after one shoot."

He was right. It wasn't Vogue. But it was a start.

Also, I recalled, I had categories listed on my website, there were a few, but no fashion. It hadn't really been my thing.

"So?"

"Eh?"

"Are you doing it?"

"Of course. June."

"Wow, just two weeks from now?"

"Yeah…" Damn, I'd have to figure out what to do with the studio.

As though he'd read my mind yet again, Miles asked "What will you do with the studio?"

It was, on the one hand, a very good, very peaceful thing, on the other hand utter shit to be, like, 97 % friendless. Greg and Phoebe and Miles were working. I squinted at Ben. Ben was going to be busy working, and schooling. And being sixteen. So no.

"How long will you be gone?" Ben asked.

"Just a week". A week was manageable. I'd put the information on my site. And there were always bakeries and boutiques with signs that read "closed from date x – date y for personal reasons" etc..

I popped the remaining piece of bread into my mouth and made to answer the E-Mail before another semi-acceptable fashion photographer in the making came along.

"Dear Millie……"

Lynne, 1998

"I'm starting to worry about you." Cam said tearfully as I emerged from the toilet cabin, a shivery mess that smelled of puke.

Me too. I thought. I'd thought was getting better, that it had been one of those disgusting one day flu things where you're either on or over the loo all night and awake in the morning after two hours of sleep feeling like new. But a few days later, in the middle of Maths class, it had started again.

"What if you've got stomach cancer or something?"

"I've not." Though I couldn't blame it on fishfingers this time. There hadn't been any lunch yet and all I'd had was jam-toast. What had there even been inside me that could turn into that much puke?

"Let's tell your fosterdad. He'll let you go home."

I shook my head. I didn't want to have to tell Greg I felt sick again nor did I want to phone Phoebe.

"We've got five more hours of school to go, Lynne!"

"I'll go to the nurse." I mumbled and walked along the corridor. "You go back to class."

She stood and looked back and forth between me and the other end of the hall where the classroom was, nodded curtly and left me alone. Poor Cam. I knew how she worried, but I couldn't face someone cooing and flapping over me, no matter how much I adored both my best friend and my foster parents.

The school nurse asked the same questions Dr. Whatsisname had. Diarrhea? No. Throwing up? Yes, a lot of that lately.

"For how long have you felt sick?" she asked as she felt my forehead and reached for the thermometer. "Threw up once. Then four days not. Then once again right now." I felt very tearful suddenly. This was very horrible. I didn't like talking about intimate things like that.

"Are you on any medication at all?"

"No. I think."

"Last period?"

"Eh, why?" I blushed violently, though I'd been white as a sheet in the toilet mirror.

"Just a standard question."

I thought about it. I didn't have one of those menstruation-diaries some of the girls talked about to keep track.

"About five weeks ago? Six?"

"Ah, so you're a bit late." She looked at me thoughtfully.

Late? For class? Or what?

"Have you ever been to a gynecologist?"

"No..." I didn't like where this was going one bit. Phoebe had asked me the same just recently and all she'd said was she'd have to try and get me an appointment. I could imagine nothing worse than having a stranger, male or female, poking around in my private parts with metal devices while commenting on them.

She had a round, pretty face with kind little wrinkles around her eyes and emitted a motherly warmth. And so I didn't hate her for suggesting this. "What do you think is wrong?"

She looked mildly irritated at why I didn't know what she was on about, but it dawned on me when, subconsciously, her eyes briefly averted downward in the direction of my belly.

"Oh you mean…but…" I stammered and blushed once more.

"It's alright. Go home for now and lie down. Try a cup of fennel tea and get your fostermum to make an appointment."

"I mumbled my thanks and left, but waited outside to get Cam between classes.

When she finally got out, she came running towards me and looked at me expectantly. "Why are you still here?"

I looked into her wide, worried doe-eyes and swallowed the tears that had begun to well in my own.

"She thinks I could be pregnant…" I said when I was sure no one could hear.

Her eyes grew even wider. "What? But surely…"

My face cringed.

"Alan Johnson?"

I nodded again.

"You've been bumping uglies?!"

I nodded curtly and looked down at the floor like a child that was admitting to having drawn on the wall with felt pens.

She mouthed an "oh my god" and theatrically placed her hand over her mouth.

"Where? When? HOW? Like, was he ontop or..."

I felt weary and tired and tearful and not capable of answering questions exactly as to where or when or especially how the occurrence had occurred right now. Or ever.

"I just want to go and find out if I even am later on and then worry about shit like that."

She looked half disappointed, half accepting, and embraced me before we walked off to our next lesson. I felt well enough to get through a few more hours.

After school I began to panic. When reality had sunk in and I commenced mentally bashing my stupid, immature head against a solid, unmoving object.

It was only once, what could possibly happen? What indeed, bloody Idiot. Fuck. Shit. Arse.

For once I was very happy about the fact that Greg left earlier than I did half the time and therefore couldn't give me a lift. It would have made an awkward sitting in the car in silence yet more awkward because I knew something he didn't and, if the nurse's assumption was the case he would have to know. And Phoebe. And the rest of the world. My small world that was. That would be pure shit. Real, proper, stinky crap.

Not only that, they would have to know about the occurrence: that I'd had had intercourse with a male human being. That I'd been rolling around naked on a bed making primitive, involuntary noises with a weird face. Even I was disgusted at myself.

Alan, I had to tell him. The idiot. Ok, slow down. Step one: go to Boots, get a test.

So there I was a few minutes later, infront of the local drugshop when a new wave of hot, sweaty panic came over me accompanied by nausea. What was I supposed to do? Just...go in and grab a test and lay it on the counter? Was that weird? I mean, they were there. To buy. So obviously I wouldn't be the first female to enter the shop and get one. SO I took a deep breath and reemerged yet another five minutes later with a four pound 69 (how ironic) pregnancy test and – I was hoping these would take the focus off it – a bottle of travel-shampoo and a packet of vegetarian wine gums. I hated wine gums.

I was greeted warmly by Phoebe as usual. I had our usual "how was your day, Love?" conversation with her and was just about to go to the loo when, as if she'd smelled it, the door rang and Phoebe let Cam in. "Just so we could look over our French homework together."

"Well, it's good if someone can make her do her French. Will you stay for tea?"

We went to the upstairs bathroom together. Cam wanted to come in too, but discretely waited outside after I'd asked if we could please not be that type of woman. Hadn't she been aware of the state I was currently in she might have been huffy, but she was perfectly patient.

I felt stupid, peeing on this little stick of plastic while my heart was racing and my hands were trembling (which made it hard to aim). So there I sat. And waited.

Lynne, 2016

I came home from my dinner at Greg an Phoebe's that Friday and just about fainted. Coming home and Mile's being in the flat was one thing. Even Miles plus one was alright.

Miles plus one plus about ten more, however, without being warned was not my idea of ok.

An abundance of people, male and female, aged somewhere between mid-twenties to mid-thirties, talking and laughing and drinking to loud rave music.

"Miles! What the fuck!?" I attempted to shout, without success.

I put my bag down and ignored the people looking up, mild interest crossing their face before they returned to their conversation and/or coke and rum.

He was perched on the arm of the armchair, Sam curled up beside him, looking like crap.

"What's all this?" I mouthed at Miles and gestures at the people and the booze and the crisps scattered across the floor.

"Sam isn't feeling very well, so I threw a bit of a party to cheer him up!"

This was so Miles. "Hope that's ok with you?"

I hesitated, then rolled my eyes and nodded.

He gave me thumbs up and then ascended from his visibly uncomfortable position to put the music down. The people stopped in mid sentenced, looking around the room as if to say "oi, where's the music gone?!"

"Everybody! This is my friend, roomy and former boss, Lynne!" I felt myself blush as I waved briefly. "Erm, hiya, everybody."

"Hi", "Hi, Lynne!" they shouted, some of their voices slightly slurred. Someone patted me on the back. "Everybody" seemed nice enough.

The music was turned back on and the party was continued.

I huddled up next to Sam and gave his shoulder an awkward pat. "What's up, Mate?"

"Aw, Lynne." Sam sighed. He looked tired and slightly broken. Not his usual quirky self. Miles had only meant the very best, but his party-strategy didn't seem to be working all that well. "I think it might be over with Pat."

"What? Why?"

He muttered something but I could hardly hear him through the loud music and chattering.

"Kitchen!" I shouted and gestured to the door Miles was just coming through with a new packet of salt'n vinegar crisps.

"Sorry?" I said once we were in the kitchen and a good bit of the noise was blocked out. "It's been going on for a few weeks. I've been a terrible git, being all offended and defensive when Pat came home from work all stressed out and just needing peace and quiet." He rambled on while examining a bottle containing some raspberry schnapps or other. "I took it all personally and he'd get cross and I just decided to leave earlier today." He sighed. "Aw, Lynne, what do you think, was I too hard on him? Or am I being too hard on myself?"

He looked at me with his puppy-eyes. He was obviously more than slightly pissed and it broke my heart to see him like this. The fact that - although the two of us couldn't be more different from one another - I saw myself in him right then played a relevant part in this apart from me genuinely adoring him.

I thought for a minute while pulling myself onto the worktop to be more comfortable. He did the same and so we sat next to each other for a while. "You know, I just need to feel loved and…and *wanted*. Something I haven't felt since Pat's started the new job."

I nodded while he took a swig of bourbon straight from the bottle (I hoped this didn't mean he was planning on draining it).

"Then again," he smiled sadly. "I never stop going on and on and on and…you get the idea. It must be tiring."

"You're being too hard on both of you. Pat and yourself."

He considered this for a minute. "Maybe. I don't know."

I didn't either, really. But I did know something.

"It's not always easy. We're all different, and we're all complicated."

He nodded once more, taking another swig. "Slow down! But trust me, if you feel Pat's really worth it you should try to get past this. You might be thankful you did in a few months or even years time."

Sam thought about it for a minute and then smiled. "Yeah, you might be right, Lynne."

"Of course you have to make your own decision."

"I will, but you're right and I think I'll give it another chance if Pat wants to. I do love him to bits, after all. And he's dead sexy." I smiled back. That was more like the Sam I knew.

"Mind if I crash here tonight though?" he hiccupped daintily (there was no other word to describe it).

"Of course. You're not going anywhere like that!" he laughed as we hopped off the worktop and then gave me a huge bear-hug and a kiss on the cheek.

"Thanks, Lynne. You're a lovely girl."

"I'm sooo glad you got Sam to reconsider the whole thing." Miles said after everybody had left, leaving the flat in a bit of a state. To my surprise, I discovered that I'd had fun.

It was three a.m. and a very tipsy Sam was lying in Miles' bed, leaving the sofa for Miles to sleep on.

We were sitting watching some late night shopping channel and munching the remains of a crisps-packet. I nodded. "Would've been a shame."

"Yeah, Sam and Pat are great."

"It was really nice of you to do that for him. I didn't think you were a party type."

"I'm not really. I prefer just going out with one or two mates for a pint and then coming home at one. But hey. Sam is very much a party type and I figured that's what pals are for."

"Yeah…"

He nudged me gently. "Just like you helped me out with my financial situation after he moved out." He winked. I suddenly felt slightly guilty. "Thanks, Miles. Really, you saved my arse a bit there."

"I didn't mean it that way, only kidding."

"Yeah, but still."

He put his arm round me, clumsily as his system was still in the process of breaking down three different kinds of alcohol - and gave me a bit of a squeeze.

"Thank you too. I like having you around." He looked at me calculating, then leaned in slowly and gave me a kiss. Not a kiss on the cheek like Sam, but a proper one.

He pulled back after a few seconds and after a moment of awkward sincerity, we both started to giggle. "What was that?" I asked and could tell he wasn't offended in the slightest.

"Oh, just…caught up in the moment I suppose."

I pushed him over playfullf and reached for the tv remote and looked for another channel.

"Lynne?"

"Yeah?" oh, dear. I didn't know how I'd feel about him making this an issue…

"I'm sorry to say, but I just realized you're not really my type." He winked.

"Wow, surprise!" I winked back. "I'm sorry to say, but the feeling's mutual."

I leaned back on him and felt absolutely at ease. Miles would make someone very happy some day. But, I realized once more, my heart still belonged to someone else. (I hoped that, one day, I'd be free to give someone as lovely as Miles a chance...)

Lynne, 2016 (a week later)

I entered our flat and exhaled audibly when I dropped my bag on the floor. What a week it had been! I felt like I'd been on the other side of the world and my heart felt like it might explode with happiness and pride.

I went to the kitchen and made myself a cup of coffee, then sat down and turned on the TV set but didn't really pay attention.

I was dwelling on the thoughts of the past week. It was like I'd been in the sun so much I'd tanked a lifetime of endorphins and was just constantly smiling.

I'd worked with interesting people and had, according to them, done good work and was going to be hired again. Not only that, but I'd gotten a lot of free time to pursue images of my own, private interests and caught myself photographing with the passion I'd had all those years back and remembered, with a pang of nostalgia, the afternoon Greg had pointed out the squirrel and the little bird chasing about the garden. The sea. The scenery. The smells. The evenings with people – tourists and visitors and natives, men women kids and everything in between – eating and drinking and laughing and dancing – and had realized once more that some things were too much, too vivid and too intense for even the most exclusive panorama lenses and programs to convey.

I remembered that I'd written Ben an E-Mail saying I'd meet him that afternoon at our café. And so I got myself tidied up to a point where I wasn't stinking of sweat or feeling greasy the way you do when having travelled for the better part of a day and left. He wanted to hear all about it as he hadn't just not been abroad, the poor lad had never been so much as to another part of Britain. Also, I wanted to know how his first week at work had been. I was genuinely curious, as I couldn't picture him really, actually working. Going up to the tables and giving out menus and telling folks what the daily soup and sandwich was. He was more the…bad tempered, laconic, running away from home type of kid. But then, so was I, I was coming to realize. And I was working. Boy was I working! In Greece! For a magazine!

Right, enough of that.

I arrived at the café. It was cosy. Comfortable, squishy settees up at rustic wooden tables. It was self service, but they had nice coffee and nice cakes for acceptable prices. And – I'd decided – it was getting better financially. And hopefully it would keep going that way. So I was going to treat us to not only a plain coffee and hot chocolate, but a nice millionaires shortbread or cupcake as well. So there you go, bankruptcy. That's you beat for now!

It was half past four. Twenty to. Damn, I really needed to get a mobile. In fact, I was getting one. Today. Or tomorrow.

Where was Ben? Had something happened at work? I was getting nervous. Maybe he`d forgotten. I recalled that he was, after all, though one of my closest friends, a teenage boy. And being that much older, I felt sort of responsible for him and his well being and couldn't help worrying, like an older sister or auntie would (I presumed, as I was neither I biological older sister or auntie. Probably.)...

So eventually, I got up from my squishy seat. Little John's was only a few minutes away.

I'd probably bump into him on the way and if not…I'd just wait in front of Little John's til he came out and if not…well, I'd go home and have some deep-frozen chips and see if Miles was in yet.

Ours ways failed to cross. I reached Little John's and there, outside the pub, were two people. Male, one young, the other middle aged, speaking in raised voices. One of them, the older man, seemed to be drunk. He was gesticulating wildly and wasn't speaking clearly. Oh, I hoped there wasn't going to be a big fight. I got closer and realized the kid was an employee, probably asking the drunk to leave because he was becoming rude or ranting abuse at the TV at the bar. A few steps later I realized that the kid was Ben. And he didn't seem like someone who was politely asking a drunk to leave the pub. He was upset. Not crying, but on the verge of tears. I was too far away to hear everything that was said, only singly words uttered by Ben. "Dad!" was one of them. "How can you..." his hands flew up to his head in frustration. Passers by had slowed down and were looking, some with obvious concern, some with interest. Rude buggers, I thought about the latter. Mind your own business.

Another man came out. It was Al. I felt my knees go weak and put my hand against a wall for support and stopped in my tracks.

He'd put a hand on Ben's shoulder to calm him down. Ben shouted "just go!" at the drunken man, who shook his head clumsily and did as he was told. Al and Ben spoke quietly for a few more minutes, then went back inside. What had that all been about? Dad? Had that been Ben's real, actual Dad that was, at least partly, responsible for him landing in care?

What had happened to that poor kid? I thought, a great sadness rising in my chest.

He came out, his work clothes exchanged for a normal t- shirt, and was coming in my direction. Shit. I leaned against the wall in what I hoped was a casual pose, like I'd just been waiting. God I wished I had one of those fancy smartphones right now. I could pretend I was scrolling up and down on facebook or listening to music. All casual. Like you do.

"Lynne!"

"What the fuck was that?"

Way to be subtle...

"Umm..."

"Sorry but..."

"I don't care what your heard. I don't want to talk about that bloody arsehole."

Ben pushed past me and quickened his step. I was sure I'd heard him choke on his last word. I suppressed the impulse to run after him. I knew what it was like when people went after you trying to calm you down and get you to talk.

I felt sad. I'd really been looking forward to seeing him. Then I felt sad because my new best friend was a sixteen year old boy that studied English literature. But so what. At least he wouldn't fuck any of my ex-lifepartners. Maybe.

So instead of the café, I went to the supermarket for some bread and cheese and went home. I'd been tempted to buy a nice bottle of sparkling wine to celebrate with Miles, but decided it was best for everyone until I felt absolutely sure I wouldn't get sick again…It was like Cam with one of her refined sugar withdrawals to "stop the cravings". I felt a stab of pain and tears shot to my eyes as I suddenly pined for my friend and to tell her all about my adventures on Crete. I wanted to hug her, cry on her, and…and what, say sorry? Hear her sorry? Say nothing at all? But it would be there, between us, forever. I could never look her in the eye and genuinely love and trust her again, could I? I was sure of it. And the thought of that seemed more painful than that of not seeing her at all.

I went home and found Miles already there, watching TV.

"Thought you were meeting your boyfriend?"

"Yuck?!"

"Brought the kid for tea?"

"No."

I reluctantly told him what I'd seen and how he'd pissed off.

Miles gave me a one armed hug. "I know you really care about the wean. But don't fret about it. He's working, and living by himself, he's not yours to worry about."

"I know." But who's was Ben to worry about if not mine? I cut a slice of cheddar off the block and munched away at it while trying to figure out where I'd seen that actor before.

Miles was right. Ben was a big lad with a job and stuff. When I was his age I'd survived God knows what kind of crap and here I was. Still, I made a mental note to go and see him at work. Al was the chef after all and would be in the kitchen and I wouldn't have to stand the sight of his face. That kid really needed a bloody phone. How to be a hypocrite, step one…

Al, 2016

I looked at my watch for the fifth time that morning. We'd started doing breakfasts to expand the spectrum of our customers and Ben had been due at eight to start getting everything set. It was ten to nine, where was the kid? I knew about his situation and was seriously debating giving him a pay-raise or getting him a cheap mobile myself, it was impossible to contact him. Also, I was starting to rather like the kid and was beginning to worry about him. Trisha, the other waitress, entered the kitchen, flustered. She got flustered very quickly.

"Mr. Johnson? Why aren't the tables set for breakfast? Wasn't Ben coming to do that? We're about to open."

"It's Al, Trisha. He was supposed to, but he's not here. Would you mind?"

She nodded and started to gather cutlery and napkins.

I left the kitchen. Maybe he'd turned up late and was getting a hard time from Alex, who fancied himself a sort of manager-of-everyone.

But no. Alex was looking at the clock, looking flustered himself, while getting the coffee machine started. But no Ben.

I looked outside. Still no Ben. Just three customers waiting to have breakfast. A couple and a woman with blonde hair who's silhouette looked oddly familiar.

"Alex, would you open up, please? Trisha's here, she'll manage the first few customers until rush-hour."

"I'll give Anna a call in a minute, maybe she can come now instead of Tuesday. The poor girl will have to be taken to hospital hyperventilating if she's left alone." He added, glancing at Trisha frantically collecting a bundle of forks she'd dropped while trying to hurry.

"Leave her, she's only young."

Alex opened up and the customers came in.

I knew it! What was she doing here? Should I talk to her? Was she here to batter my head in because of Cam?

Trisha went to the couple nervously and handed them the menus.

I'd have to go back to the kitchen in a minute, but I wanted to wait and see what she was doing here. Did she need my help? Would I give it to her? Of course I would. It was Lynnette Wilson. The tall blonde girl that had stood up to the bullies.

I felt like a schoolboy, hiding beside the coffee machine so your crush wouldn't see you and talk to you even though you wanted nothing more in the whole world.

She looked well..nice..I wondered whether she'd gotten rid of her drinking problem and longed suddenly to present my new, clean self to her. Even if she wasn't dry…how I wished we'd found another way. We hadn't broken each other, after all. We'd broken ourselves.

It hadn't been a vicious circle. It had been our own weakness. And fear, and trying to escape from fear and from facing reality, and facing ourselves.

I heard her order plain black coffee, and then ask Trish if Ben was there. Lynne knew Ben? How did Lynne know Ben?

Trisha said no. Well, yes, of course she could have plain black coffee, but no, Ben wasn't there. Sorry.

Lynne looked at her watch, worried. She got up, scratched her head, as if she didn't really know what to do.

"I'll get her's" I said to Trish. I got a cup and made a cup of coffee, placed it on a saucer and, after hesitating, carried it over to Lynne. She just about jumped out of her skin when I approached her and placed her hand on her chest.

"Hi…"

"Hi."

Yep, still felt like a teenager.

"This is on the house."

"Ok."

She took it, took a gulp and burnt her tongue.

"You ok?"

She nodded with tears in her eyes.

I wished I could say something. But what?

"You look well." That's what you said, wasn't it?

"Thanks." Then, "do you know where Ben might be? He's a friend of mine and he works here and he was in a fizz yesterday and I'm worried."

I was slightly overwhelmed. Nothing except "Hi" and "ok" for nearly two years and then all those words. So lynne-ish. I felt my fondness for her rushing back..this girl was something else.

But I had to keep it light. Knowing her, there was no chance. Everything that had happened and not happened was mostly my fault after all.

"No. He was supposed to be here an hour ago. Doesn't have a phone, so.."

"No, doesn't have a phone."

"Should we…I mean, he's usually so reliable."

"I'll go by his flat."

"Don't you have to work?" Shit, too personal.

"Closed today."

"Alright."

Alex, who'd inevitably overheard some of the conversation, said "you go out to look for him, I've got this sorted."

Alex was a bossy boots, but he was a fine cook, so I removed my shirt and got my jacket. "Let's go then."

She rolled her eyes, but said "ok."

So she didn't want me to go. But Ben was my employee and he was a teenager and anything could have happened between yesterday afternoon and now. And also…I had things to say to Lynne. I didn't know what, and I felt like an arsehole and a coward for not at least trying to contact her all this time…Then again, we'd been separated for two years after all..but before that we'd been together for the best part of a decade.

She didn't talk, but that was natural for Lynne, not to talk.

"What have you been doing?"

Smooth, man, smooth…

"What?"

"I mean…workwise and…"

"Oh. Well, I was broke, but you know that. Moved in with a friend now and was in Crete doing a shooting."

"Wow, Crete? That's where you got the tan."

Was that the ghost of a smile I just saw? Maybe I should shut up.

"I've got a website now. And a phone. Since yesterday."

"Really? Wow, look who's up to date!"

She smiled. She didn't look at me, but she smiled, with teeth and all, and blushed slightly.

It was fascinating...People grew up physically. They got jobs, maybe even their own business with employees and equiptent etcetera. Some of them might be right arseholes if they had the power. Grumpy bosses sitting behind their desks, giving trainees hell for coming to work in sneakers, sitting on the bus tutting because a kid's laughing loudly. We start to think about all these serious things. Work, finances. Furniture. We start to fight about bigger things than toy cars. About girls, about money, about countries and resources. We become more careful in our actions because we start to realize we're not immortal. But I thought at that moment, walking beside Lynne feeling all smug because I'd made her laugh while feeling upset...that it doesn't matter really whether you're fifteen or fifty five. We're still the same person, really. It's what happens to us during all those years that makes us happier or grumpier or nicer or meaner. But we still feel the same joy when we see Tom and Jerry's on, we still want our Mum when someone's left us, our heart still beats harder when we accidentally touch that girl's hand while walking beside her.

"There it is."

It was a small building complex. It looked habitable. We got inside and went up the staircase past several doors, nearly bumping into a pair of teenagers on the way, until Lynne stopped in front of one. She exhaled audibly. I could sense she was scared. I heard voices from inside.

He probably had a hangover and was puking his guts out or had forgotten to set his alarm. It happened.

Lynne, 2016

I lifted my hand carefully to ring the doorbell. I was shaking slightly. Whether it was from seeing Al and having to control feelings I couldn't even begin to interpret or whether I was simply worried sick about Ben I didn't know.

The voices came closer and a boy about Ben's age with dark hair and bright green eyes opened the door. He looked pale and frightened.

Another boy was frantically knocking at a door in the background I supposed lead to the bathroom.

"Hi, we're looking for Ben." I said, my voice shaking.

"We don't know what's wrong. I wanted to go to the toilet about half an hour ago and the door wouldn't open. Ben was totally pissed last night got up sometime earlier, I think to be sick. We're worried he's choked."

"Have you called someone?"

The boy shook his head. "We were just going to smash the door in."

"I'll phone the emergency doctor." Said Al and got his mobile out.

I started hammering at the door myself. "BEN!"

Silence.

"Shit, he's dead." The boy with blonde hair wailed. "We shouldn't have let him drink so much. He was really upset about something."

The other boy was white as a sheet and just kept mumbling "Fuck." Under his breath.

I was shaking all over. This couldn't be happening. I felt Al's arms around me but other than that, everything was a blur. The emergency doctor arrived fully equipped and smashed the bathroom door in, and sure enough, there he was lying rolled up on the floor beside the toilet which emitted a smell of sick.

"Is he dead?" I heard the blond boy ask, his voice squeaking.

The doctor who had been feeling his pulse shook his head. "No, but he's out cold. How much did he have to drink?"

"A lot." The boy said, colour returning to his face. "Too much. We're sorry."

"He'll have alcohol-poisoning. Let's get him out, quick."

Feeling returned to my trembling limbs as they carried Ben out of the bathroom on a stretcher, covered up as he was under cooled.

I collapsed onto the small sofa beside the dark-haired boy who was now sobbing, his thin body heaving, unable to cry myself with shock.

"Lynne. Lynne!" Al was shaking my shoulders but I felt unable to do more that look at the wall behind him. He was alive.

I pulled myself together. I felt a little bit bad about leaving the two frightened boys alone, but I figured they would be alright. Ben needed us now. He needed me now.

We sat beside him in the back of the ambulance, me holding his pale, cold, lanky hand in my own.

He looked so fragile lying there, unconscious, his dark hair falling across his eyes like it did. I was willing him with all my might to be ok.

Al just sat and looked at him, a little crease of worry having formed on his brow. He then looked up at me. And put his hand on top of mine. A little, cynical voice inside me tutted and rolled it's eyes. Could it get any more cheesy than this? If I wrote a book about this, readers would merely shake their heads and mutter "what bullshit" under their breath while throwing it in the nearest train-station-bin.

I met his eyes briefly for the first time in two years and he gave me a reassuring little smile. I averted my eyes, but felt his gaze resting on me. Could we arrive already?

What the fuck was this anyway? We hadn't so much as exchanged a friendly nod in the supermarket for nineteen months and there we were, holding an unconscious teenager's hand and each others in the back of an ambulance. I wasn't good at stuff like this, but this shit was proper scary.

We arrived at the hospital and Ben was swiftly carried inside by the emergency doctor and the nurse.

We were asked several questions, explained Ben's current situation about living on his own etc. and then had to wait, as we were not his parents or guardians.

We just sat. Al looked at his phone now and again and otherwise took to tapping his foot and drumming his fingers in a nervous sort of way. I finally cleared my throat and said hoarsely "go back to work."

I saw his sideways glance out f the corner of my eye and could swear he looked hurt.

"I'll be alright. Just want to see he's ok and Alex is taking care of things."

"I nodded."

I wanted him to go. It had been enough drama and enough ex-life-partner for one day and I didn't know what to feel and so my body decided to go into sleep-mode. I simply felt nothing, though an unpleasant pressure was building up somewhere behind my face. I didn't want to see him any more!

"So."

"So."

"How do you know the kid, then?"

I explained briefly that he'd run away, he'd been in to visit me here and there and I felt comfortable in his company. I didn't have many people I could turn to after...

I gave myself a fright when I realized in which direction the conversation was starting to go and pretended to be choking on my saliva. Had he bought it? No. Of course not. He was blushing violently.

"Lynne –"

"No!" that had been a tad too harsh. "No. Please."

As if someone had sensed that I really needed something like this to happen, the door of the surgery opened and a doctor emerged, followed by a two male nurses pushing a bed with a drip beside it.

"Is he ok?" it burst out of me.

"We've pumped his stomach and he should be just fine. We're transporting him to a ward where he can wake up. I'd like to keep him in to be sure, though. You're his parents?

"I'm his boss but I think my friend should go and sit with him." Al said as he got up.

"Alright, this way then."

I looked back at Al, who just gave a weak smile and waved awkwardly. I said "thanks", because it was the right thing to do and regardless of all my other…feelings…whatever they were, I was thankful.

It was quiet on the ward.

I sat...the numbness left my body...oh why...and I sat. And I felt. And I cried. I put my head down in the mattress so my head nuzzled Ben's side and cried until I felt like I couldn't anymore, then I cried more. It was so cliché, I thought these things just happened in dramatic hospital TV series, but I don't know how much time had passed when I heard a weak groan and Ben moved. I looked up in time to see his sticky eyes open slowly. He focused and looked at me, but seemed unable to speak.

"Hi."

"I feel like shit."

"You look like shit."

He closed his eyes again and we didn't say anything for some time. I just held his hand and was so relieved and happy when he squeezed it reassuringly. Then I felt stupid because Ben was the one that had probably nearly kicked the bucket while lying in his own puke and who knows what else after all and he felt the need to make a gesture to comfort me.

Ben, 2016

After staying for two nights "for observation", feeling like absolute hell the whole time, I got to go home. Except I didn't want to go home. Not that I disliked Will and George.

But I felt the need to be with someone I'd known for a while and really trusted. The thing was, I didn't only feel like shit physically, but emotionally as well. I felt like a right wiener, but everything just came flooding in that evening I'd just about killed myself. Not that I'd wanted to, mind. Kill myself, that is. I just wanted to not feel.

As it was no option for me going back to Ann's and there was no chance on me voluntarily going near that asshole again, and not having anyone really close apart from Lynne (I generally didn't like or trust people very much, which, in my opinion, no one could judge me for considering the shit that had happened throughout my childhood), I'd said yes, please to Lynne's offer of me staying with her and Miles until I felt up to anything apart from existing.

To my surprise, it wasn't Lynne or Miles who was waiting for me outside the hospital when I came out, but Alan.

My first thought was, WTF? But he waved when he spotted me and so, I approached him.

"Hi there, kid."

"Hi."

"I talked to Lynne and as I have a car and she doesn't, I'd get you and take you to your place for some stuff then drive you over. Is that ok?"

I must have taken on a rather skeptical expression, as he chuckled nervously and said "I won't kidnap you or anything. I could have done that during the past three weeks you've been working for me."

I brightened up then. It was very nice considering he had nothing to do with me, really. "Ok. Yeah. Thanks."

He scratched his head nervously when we approached his rather small, rather shabby looking vehicle. "When I said car, I meant this thing. But, you know, it drives. So…" Still, the car looked better than I felt.

He let me out at the student's home and I packed a rucksack with some clothes, my wallet etc., explained to my roomies where I'd be and went back to the car.

I still felt a bit awkward being driven around by my boss, whom I hardly knew, but it was fine. He didn't ask any awkward questions just to fill the silence.

He dropped me off and asked for me to take it easy and to let him know when I felt up to working, then left.

I rang and Miles opened the door, ruffled my hair (a gesture that seemed a bit funny considering he was about five years older than me, but I still appreciated it).
I went upstairs and inside their flat and Lynne jumped up from the sofa to give me a hug. "Hi."
"Hi."
I was so touched by this genuine gesture of kindness that I felt tears welling up behind me eyes and quickly let go.
"Want a sandwich?"
I nodded. I was starving.
When we all had a sandwich and a drink on the coffee table in front of us, Lynne gingerly, obviously not wanting me to get

angry, asked "what was new". I saw no need to be angry and also felt it would be highly inappropriate, I told her about my social worker's visit. She'd strongly recommended I start a weekly therapy session and might need meds for depression and stuff. I was considering the therapy thing but I didn't feel like taking anti-depressants in order to cope with life. I'd rather just try to cope. I didn't know.

Lynne put her cheese sandwich down and sighed when Miles got up to answer the phone.

"Why would you do that?"

"What?"

"You know…"

I knew exactly. I just didn't know how to put it in words.

"I didn't want to feel."

She didn't say anything. Just looked at her sandwich. I could tell she was strongly debating on whether or not to say what was on her mind.

Then she started to speak. "I didn't want to feel for a while either. I really badly didn't want to feel and it made everything worse. Sometimes you have to feel to be able to deal with things. Don't do that again. Don't be me."

She was looking at me now. She'd never really looked me in the eye before.

Miles came back and recommenced eating his sandwich. "That was Bigg, have to do the early shift tomorrow."

I then realized something. "Lynne, why aren't you at work?"

To my horror, she smiled, then tears started to run down her face.

"Er…"

"It's ok."

"...Er..."

"Lynne put the place up for rent two days ago."

"Oh..." she'd talked about it. She knew it was really inevitable but loved that place more than anything.

"Yeah. For now at least..." she sniffed and wiped her eyes.

"But...what are you going to do?"

Her smile turned from sad to happy and she said "*Nostalgie* liked my work."

I knew, of course, this meant Lynne would be away more often. But I couldn't remember ever having felt so genuinely happy for someone in my life. I knew what it was like to go through hell and something told me so did she. If anyone deserved this kind of break I knew it was Lynne.

And then I remembered something else. Something I'd failed to question earlier. "Do you know Alan?"

"Erm…I suppose?"

"Like, before…that happened though, I mean."

Of course they'd been in contact while I was in hospital, him being my boss and her a friend. But the way he'd spoken about her as "Lynne" made me feel that, unless they'd developed a friendship and were on personal terms while I was half unconscious, that they must know each other.

"Erm…I suppose."

She was anxious about something. She was blushing and taking extra big mouthfuls of sandwich, so as not to have to talk.

Miles scratched the back of his head and excused himself to go to the bathroom. I knew then I should probably shut up.

"Sorry."

She chewed and swallowed. Then examined the remains of her lunch for a minute and answered without looking up. "I was with him for a while."

"Oh. Ok. Really?"

I was startled and didn't bother to hide it. I found this rather amusing and ironic, two of the few people I had to do with on a weekly basis apart from roomies and college-mates having made out. Disgusting, come to think of it.

"How long?"

"Twelve years."

She turned on the TV and I could tell she wished to end the conversation. I took the hint and shut the F up.

I resumed my studying and my work at Little John's a week later and moved back home to my flat in St. Andrew's.

I was due to start therapy in another weeks time. No meds for now. But I'd see how things went. I went over to Lynne's studio to help clear out her things. Apparently someone was going to open a giftshop.

But another shock was about to come. I was at home studying when there was a knock at the door and Sandra O'Connor stood there, her bag in one hand, two sealed letters in the other.

"Wha-"

"Can I come in?"

I stepped aside and let her enter. She sat down on the sofa (we had no such thing as a dining table). I got these letters addressed to you. They're from-"

"Him?"

...

"Are they from him?"

"From your adoptive-father, yes.

"He's not even my father anymore. He stopped being my father the minute he dumped me for you to find another family for me." I wasn't exactly shouting, but my voice was raised. Sandra took on her sympathetic look. I was glad Will or George weren't in. I suspected they were highly uncomfortable being confronted with my difficult past. Not that I whined about it or anything but they knew what had happened since the drinking affair. I'd never really had a lot to drink before, so evidently, they'd known something was the matter.

"Just...Maybe you should just read them anyway."

I nodded reluctantly. What could that prick possibly have to say to me?

"Do you want me to stay while…"

I shook my head a little too violently.

"No thanks." She nodded understandingly, a trace of hurt flashing across her face, and got up to leave. Boy, the things social workers had to go through. "Thanks though, Sandra."

I owed her that much. She smiled then and told me to let her know if I needed anything.

I felt like I'd made such progress. After Lynne had gotten on my nerves, I'd actually gotten a pay as you go phone. I'd had my hair cut and, while liking the fringe swooping over my face, had it shortened enough to be able to see three dimensionally. I met a girl at college I found semi-attractive with big brown eyes and a gorgeous smile. I couldn't really remember ever having found anything or anyone optically appealing, which the other guys seemed to find un-normal. I supposed I'd always been busy dealing with other stuff rather than drooling over some horrid girl's racks. But it wasn't her rack, it was (please excuse me for sounding ridiculous) her *soul* that was hot. Or her aura or whatever you wished to call it. Just her as a person.

I was still trying to pluck up the courage to ask her if she wanted to have lunch together sometime. Just not right now.

I felt better and more mature. And so, I decided maybe I should have a look at what Quentin had to say. Just not right now.

Miles was there. And a man in his fifties I didn't know who Lynne introduced as Greg. I assumed he was her former fosterdad. He was a nice, rather short man with kind, happy blue eyes. He emphasized how glad he was that Lynne had finally gotten off her high horse and accepted some help. "You'd have slipped a disc carrying this furniture around, Lynni."

She shook her head irritably at this but I could tell she adored him and was grateful that we were here to help.

While I worked my way through a box of old photos Lynne had asked me to sort out ("keep some nice ones for future applications and stuff"), I couldn't help but wonder what Lynne's story was. I knew she'd been a foster kid, too. I knew she'd run away and had ended up in a half way house until she'd "gotten herself sorted out". But she got along so well with Greg. Had they abandoned her like he'd abandoned me? Had she forgiven them? Or had she had to forgive them for something?

I stumbled across so many nice pictures, I didn't feel comfortable being in charge of throwing any of them out. But though I was a seventeen year old male I sadly lacked the physical strength Miles had to go lugging stuff around. I made a mental note to start training in some way or another.

There were some copies of family portraits and baby/toddler photo-sessions and a lot of passport photos and photo-sessions and portraits of men, women and kids of every age group. Some smiling, others sincere. Some colourful, some black and white.

There was one of a pregnant African woman sitting cross legged on the floor, facing the camera with her eyes lowered to her naked stomach, which she gingerly cupped with both hands. Another of a family. A man and a woman in their early thirties, I guessed, holding a baby that was looking into the camera with wide eyes while they looked at her, both smiling. It looked so perfect and so spontaneous at the same time.

There was one of a young woman with dark doe-eyes and dark, cropped hair looking over her shoulder, just the hint of a smile on her glossy lips and a black and white of a severe looking, shirtless, heavily tattooed man in his twenties looking straight at the camera.

The pictures told stories of people, of histories, of feelings. I didn't want to throw any out and so just ended up sorting them into categories. Families and couples, adults, babies. Black and white and colour.

A week later, Lynne was due to collect me at work. She'd just been in Edinburgh for two days on a photo shoot had said she was going to Greg and Phoebe's (Phoebe apparently being Greg's wife) and if I wanted to come.

I said yes, having rather had taken to Greg, which had happened in an astonishing frequency for me. He'd gotten us all cappuccinos to-go at the nearest coffee shop, as it was getting cold, and had made friendly conversation with me without probing. He hadn't asked stuff about my past and who exactly I was and bla, just what I did and what I studied and what it was like.

She came in like she usually did, nervously looking around for some reason and fidgeting like she couldn't wait to get outside.

Alan came out of the kitchen to talk to Alex about something in an annoyed tone of voice (Alex had ranted at Betty again for some reason, which Al strongly disliked as he disapproved of employees being ranted at. This attitude increased my respect towards him). He spotted Lynne in midsentence and his face suddenly turned calm. When he'd finished, he carefully approached her.

"Hi there."

"Hi."

"Here to see Ben?"

She nodded, looking around as if she'd never been in here before and it was a highly interesting museum of something or other.

Al nodded, slightly disappointed, and made to go back to the kitchen. Then apparently decided otherwise and turned around.

"Would you like to go for dinner?"

She looked at him directly, her lips slightly open as if she wanted to say something but didn't know what.

Was this one of those moments you were supposed to step in and save someone? *Hiya, Pal. Ready to go? Bye Alan! See you Sunday, Buddy!* And swiftly drag her outside?

Or should I just resume my table-scrubbing and leave them to...whatever that was.

I could hear Lynne stutter an answer. "I'm going to Greg and Phoebe's for dinner."

"Ok. Tell them I said hi."

Alan sounded disappointed and I wondered what had happened.

But to my surprise I heard Lynne say, semi-enthusiastically. "Tomorrow, maybe?"

"Oh...alright, yes. Alex will take over."

"Alright."

"Alright."

I felt it was safe then to get my rucksack and jacket and get out.

I felt the urge to tease but decided to let it be and asked what the job was like instead. Slowly, Lynne's face took on it's usual, pale-ish colour again as she talked. She said she kept hoping to meet the editor that had made it all possible sometime but something always seemed to get in the way.

"Lynne?"

"Yeah?"

"Miss O'Connor brought me this letter the other day."

...

"From the guy that was my adoptive dad."

"Oh?"

...

"And?"

"Haven't read it."

"Why?"

"Because it might only make it worse." I glanced over to her, waiting for her to react. To go all sympathetic-adult on me and say it might help me get over it or something. But something in her silence helped me to react. "Maybe you can read it?"

"Me? Why me? It's for you." She sounded irritated and I could understand. It was for me and I couldn't run away for ever.

Not that I felt bad for hating him. Or maybe I did?

"Well, can I read it while you're there?" I said huffily. I felt weak.

"Yes. Later."

We had a lovely dinner at Greg and Phoebe's. Phoebe was…there wasn't a better word for it…sweet. They were so nice and un-annoying that I really enjoyed having dinner there. I caught Phoebe looking at me intently once or twice, as though in recognition. I wouldn't know why though. She was a teacher...maybe she taught at one of the schools I'd used to go to? I couldn't remember her from anywhere, anyway.

Greg offered to drive us both home, but we politely declined the offer and decided to take the bus.

"What about your letter?" Lynne asked while we were on the bus. "Want to read it?"

I hesitated and felt myself going tense. There were only two other people on the bus. We had twenty minutes to go. I nodded. "Ok."

I opened it up with slightly shaky hands. I'd been carrying it around with me for whatever reason. Probably most of all because I was worried Will or George opened it by mistake.

I felt safe with Lynne sitting next to me, our shoulders just touching, and unfolded the letter.

Ben,

I know you must hate me for doing what I did. ~~After your Mum~~ after Jessie passed away I was a mess. ~~It was the only right thing to do~~ I wasn't able to cope and couldn't have looked after you the way a dad should. You were only ten and needed someone to look after you properly, even if it meant you being away from home. I know we can't be a family anymore. I know I can't be your dad anymore. But I'd like it if we could talk. I'd like to know that, despite everything, you're alright. If you want, whenever you want, you're always welcome here.

Love Quentin

x

His address was scribbled on the back. The writing was slightly wonky, and I assumed he'd been intoxicated and very emotional when writing the letter. I didn't know what to feel but my chest was tightening and I felt like I had to cry but no tears were coming.

"Ok?" Lynne asked quietly. I nodded.

Lynne, 2016

That Friday evening, I felt like I was sixteen again.

Nervous, with a slightly nauseous feeling, but not the bad kind. Not entirely, at least.

Of course I was, like back then, anxious – terrified – that I'd do or say something utterly stupid and send him running. Something I never cared to feel or think with anyone else.

What was I to wear? Once again, I found myself infront of the mirror, asking myself what to wear. And once again, I found myself leaving the flat wearing my black jeans and a plain long-sleeve shirt.

Seventeen years had passed. As I locked the door and lit my cigarette, I found myself breaking it down to approximately two-hundred and four months. Round about eight hundred weeks. Many days and many, many hours. But what had changed, really? I looked a bit older. I'd learned the one thing or the other. But that feeling as I walked towards "Little John's" to meet Alan Johnson, the lanky boy with the hazel eyes and dark hair and the mole on the right side of his chin, had not changed one bit.

There he was, sitting – what a surprise – at the very same table, wearing very similar clothes. How very cliché. Part of me felt like suppressing a gagging gesture, another part just…well…no, come to think of it, that's about all I felt. But that was Al. And I was in love with him. I'd never bloody well stopped being in love with that gorgeous, shy man sitting right there with his shandy, fiddling with his napkin and looking at his watch.

He looked startled, as though he'd been lost in thought, when I sat down on the chair opposite him.

"Oh, hi there."

"Hi."

"Would you like something to drink?"

"A coke?"

He got up and got me one, with ice and a lemon slice.

Then we just sat there for a few moments until Al broke the silence.

"How are you?"

I shrugged. How was I?

"I'm doing alright." I answered genuinely.

I realized it wasn't even "alright", as in "absolute shit, but I have to cope, don't I?"

"That's great. I'm so glad you've got everything under control, Lynne. I really am."

I nodded and sipped my coke. Me too. I'd even be grand, if only you were back in my life…

"And you?"

"Me?" He hadn't even been expecting the question.

"Oh, I'm fine. Business is going o.k., as you can see."

I could. There were a lot of people. He was obviously pleased, but still so modest about it. I was so happy for him.

"I'm happy for you."

"Thanks."

We looked at each other and smiled. I felt so nervous and so comfortable around this man at the same time. It felt like he was, as was I, the very same person. Just a few years older and a few years wiser. A few years more careful.

"Are you hungry?"

I nodded. I was.

"Alex!"

Alex came to take our orders.

Al ordered a fish supper and I felt like a steak pie. I considered the mac and cheese with brown sauce but that would have been a tad too much, no?

We chatted lightly about work– Al's family and what friends were currently up to and the like – until the food came.

The steak pie was good, but not as good as when Al made it himself. I caught myself thinking about how the other guests were really missing out on something.

When we were done, neither of us made a move to get up and leave. We just sat there. I was still nervous but more comfortable, but always wondering. What was going to happen next? Were we just going to go home at some point as ex partners who were now on a friendly "are you free for a fish supper?" kind of basis…would he try to stop me? Would he want to talk about what had happened?

Should I make a move?

Was there any need?

I didn't know.

"Lynne?"

I snapped out of my thoughts.

I could tell he was thinking similar thoughts as he didn't seem to know what to say next.

He shook his head and averted his gaze.

"What?"

"I don't know. I just wonder…"

He leaned forward and gingerly took my hands in his.

"Me too."

My heart was beating fast now. Something was definitely happening. If not in general, then with my lady parts at least. I wanted him. In every way there was to want someone.

And then he looked me straight in the eye for the first time that evening. "I love you."

I knew he did. But just because you loved somebody didn't mean you wanted to be with them.

I nodded. I didn't trust myself to open my mouth without tearing up. I might as well accept that my current life was as good as it would get. I was pretty lucky altogether, after all, I decided.

He lowered his head in the attempt to hold my gaze. "And you? How do you feel, Lynne?"

"I..." my voice cracked. Ugh.

I felt his grip slacken. "It's alright. Whatever you're wanting to say…We're alright. I'm alright"

"No." I tightened my grip. "No. I love you too. I really, really do."

Amazingly, I was able to hold my tears back. Thank goodness for that. There was nothing worse than bawling openly in front of thirty other people.

Al smiled, relieved. I smiled.

There and then, I was sure everything was going to be alright. With Al and me, at least.

He walked me home later and gingerly kissed me, sending a sensation resembling an electric shock through my whole body.

Nothing whatsoever had changed.

Ben, 2016

I was right nervous. Not the sort of nervous like the moment Lynne took me home after I'd been "living rough" for two days. Not the kind of nervous I was before moving out and starting college.
I wasn't scared of being scolded or punished or being grounded or not getting a flat near campus.
I was scared of failing, scared of messing something up for good. But maybe it wouldn't be so dreadful, after all? Maybe it would simply be the final step in growing up, leaving everything I was behind and starting something entirely new?
I didn't know. But what I did know, what I'd known for a long time really, was that one could only affect something conditionally. Sometimes not even that.

Sometimes, things were simply the way they were and no one could influence them, no matter how much it hurt. It sucked, but that was life. And one had to live on, fight on, until the pain became bearable. It never went away, the pain. Time did not heal al wounds. But they became bearable. Just. A lesson I'd had to learn too early in life.

I was glad that Lynne was there. Miles had offered to cancel work and come along too, but I'd felt it would be wrong to overwhelm Quentin. He wasn't a bad guy, after all.

I didn't know what I was to expect. What I should hope for. What I should try to achieve.

I just felt it would have been more wrong than anything else to simply not react to his letter.

We sat in silence. Lynne, talkative as she may be, left me to my thoughts, which I was very thankful for in a way. I'd never found smalltalk very comforting. It was the presence of a person I valued and I'd grown very fond of Lynne. I hadn't been fond of anyone since my parents. Since Quentin and Jessie. After Jessie, I'd just sort of closed off to the rest of the world.

We sat on the bus in silence, both lost in our own thoughts. I hated myself for it, but a part of me couldn't help but hope the bus would have a minor accident or we'd get in a terrible traffic jam – both of which was highly unlikely – or that something, anything would happen to prevent us from going on. But the bus drove steadily on at approximately thirty miles per hour.

One stop to go. My heart started pounding. The same sensation I'd always had in school when I entered a new class for the first time and had to introduce myself.

Lynne looked at me as the bus rolled to a halt. "This the one?"

I nodded.

We got off and I took a deep breath. I hadn't really talked to him (screaming at him didn't count) for the best part of six years. Maybe I'd feel better afterwards. Who knew.

"Should I wait outside?" Lynne asked quietly and I thought about it for a minute.

"Maybe you could come with me 'til we've said hi?" I felt myself blush. I felt ridiculous, but I was suddenly ten years old again, feeling the need to hold someone's hand, at least figuratively, when in a scary situation.

After Lynne had finished her cigarette, I rang the doorbell and we waited. Perhaps he wouldn't even be home.

But he was.

The door opened and before me stood Quentin. A lanky man in his early fifties, salt and pepper hair – more salt than pepper – and dark, droopy eyes. One could tell that this was a man that had suffered in all sorts of ways. A sad, vacant gaze and worry lines betrayed his ever present pain, but still he smiled when he recognized me.

"Hi." I shuffled my feet nervously.

"Would you like to come in?"

I looked at Lynne who, I noticed, was screwing up her eyes, her head slightly cocked, as she took in Quentin's appearance.

Quentin looked startled, as though he'd noticed her standing there for the first time. He held out his hand. "Quentin Anderson. You're a friend of Ben's? Or a social worker?"

Quentin's face too took on a peculiar expression, as though he was trying to remember something.

"I…yes, I'm a friend. Lynne." She took his hand and gave it a firm shake.

"Lynne. Well, do come in and have something to drink."

We followed him inside. What a strange feeling it was to be walking through this hallway again. This place, this house, this man had been my whole childhood.

I got a quick look at the pictures hanging on the walls that led past the kitchen to the living and dining room. Photos of Quentin in his younger years with his sister and his parents. Photos of Jessie. A small, curvaceous woman with long, dark hair and kind eyes, always smiling.

Photos of me.

The three of us together. A family.

He led us to the coffee table where we sat on the old sofa, leaving the chair for Quentin. I'd been small at the time, but I remembered his always preferring the armchair to the settee.

I looked at Lynne once more. Her gaze was vacant, but she gave me a quick glance and a reassuring nudge when she noticed my gaze.

What was up with her? I was supposed to be the anxious one. But then again, that was Lynne.

Quentin came with a tray with tea and a jug of milk and some biscuits.

"I wasn't sure whether anyone likes coffee, so I thought tea would be just fine."

He set the tray on the coffee table and went over to the old wooden showcase – one of the pieces of furniture I remembered but had never really noticed as a kid – but then, to my surprise, returned after hesitating for a moment and sat down. I could tell he'd wanted to have a dram but settled for a cup of tea while we – particularly I – was there. A gesture I was very grateful for.

I'd nearly drunk myself to death to blend out the pain and the fear. I didn't want him blending out me while I was there to see him.

I realized then that I didn't want the memory of our years together – with Quentin and Jessie and me – to only be bearable after a reasonable amount of booze. For either of us.

We each got a cup of tea and put in milk and a spoonful of sugar. Quentin and Lynne didn't let each other out of their sight, which seemed a little bit awkward. What was going on?

Then everything happened really fast. All of a sudden, Lynne jumped to her feet, spilling some tea in the process, a look of panic and sheer terror on her face.

"You!" she whispered, her eyes still focused on Quentin, who's expression also turned from curiosity to recognition and then surprise. "Baker…Lynette…"

His eyes shot to me, back to Lynne, to me.

Lynne didn't seem to know what or who to look at and finally shook her head in resignation and quietly said "I… I need to go. Thanks for the tea." And to me "See you soon. I'm sorry."

got her bag and left the house.

I looked at Quentin questioningly, who gave me an apologetic look. What had just happened? Should I go after her? I assumed Lynne wasn't the type of person who liked people going after her. And also, I'd come to see Quentin. Did he know what was going on?

"Dad?"

He nodded slowly, his eyes now averted.

"I'm so glad you came to see me, Ben. I'm so sorry for everything that's happened."

There were tears in his eyes he was trying to hold back.

I nodded. I sensed somehow that I wasn't going to get anything out of him. "Me too."

We took sips of tea, had a biscuit each, and I told Quentin that I was now a college student. That I had a flat of my own – well, one third my own – and a job in a restaurant. Quentin seemed genuinely interested. "I'm proud of you. And your Mum would be so proud of you. After all you've had to go through."

I nodded, suddenly feeling shy. "Thanks."

When I was about to leave, I turned towards him once more, deciding to ask one last time
what was going on and where he knew Lynne from and what had scared her.
I knew it was probably none of my business but felt the need to know.
"Dad?"
"I know, I know. As I've noticed, you don't know what the deal is. But if you want to know what happened, you'd best ask that friend of yours. You seem to be very close." He chuckled. "How ironic. I'd really like to know how…" there was that melancholy look of resignation and – perhaps – acceptance again.
"To me, you'll always be my boy. But at the very moment, we're not very close to each other. How could it be any other way? And I hope that someday we'll be close again."

I nodded once more. "Me too." My voice cracked.

"If you want to know anything, ask her. She knows everything. You're welcome here any time."

I nodded again. I thought about giving him a hug but right now it didn't feel right just yet. I looked at him and said "o.k." and turned to leave. It was getting dark, but I decided to go by Lynne's before going back to St. Andrew's.

I found myself summing dates and ages up in my head, wondering whether Lynne and Dad could have been an item at some point and shuddered. No, it had to be something else. But what.

Lynne, 1998

Ten minutes had passed, and yet there I sat. Not frantically jumping up from the loo to ask my friend what on earth I should do, not thinking about all the possibilities I knew and didn't know about. Just sitting, letting reality and the fact that I would – one way or another – have to go through hell sink in, slowly and painfully, while Cam squeaked an anxious "are you ok, Lynne?" once in a while.

When I heard her quietly declare "Have you fainted? I'm going to get Phoebe." I snapped out of it, pulled my knickers and trousers up and opened the door.

Cam's face took on an instant look of relief, only to look anxious again two seconds later. "So?"

"So."

Her eyes widened. "Positive?"

"Positive."

"Oh…"

Oh indeed. I looked her in the eye, the question written all over my face. What the fuck should I do?

I went off sick the next day.

After spending most of the evening in my room, alone or in Cam's company, fretting over what was going to happen, we decided I should see a doctor.

That was a good start. Who knew, maybe the test had been rubbish and hadn't worked properly.

After convincing Phoebe that I had terrible stomach cramps and simply couldn't get out of bed and both of them had left for work, I made sure Mrs. Harris was in her room (she usually had breakfast early and then didn't emerge from her room - which had, for a while, been mine - again until the early afternoon when Phoebe came home from work to look after her.

She was.

I got my things and quietly left the house, then headed for the bus station.

When I left the doctor's practice two hours later (I'd found the address in a phonebook), I stood before yet another dilemma.

I had to go home, otherwise Phoebe would get home before me and realize I was gone. Then I'd have to tell the whole story, which I wasn't ready for.

On the other hand, I was sure I wouldn't be able to face anyone for the rest of the day at the very least. Should I contact one of my social workers? Would they know a solution?

Would they put me in some special home or other? I was sure I wouldn't be allowed to stay at Greg and Phoebe's...

I was old enough to leave care, but I still went to school and didn't have a job.

Surely Cam would know what to do? Or Alan?

No, not Alan. I couldn't bear to tell Alan. What would his parent's say? I didn't know them well enough to be able to anticipate a reaction of any kind.

What I needed was time. For what exactly and how much was irrelevant right now. Seemed irrelevant. Frankly, all that was going through my head at that moment was: what the bloody feck now?

I just about shit myself that night. Like, for eight hours straight, I was literally just about shitting myself.

I couldn't remember having ever been so scared. Or so cold, or so miserable.

I didn't sleep. Whether from cold or from the fear of something happening –I didn't know. Probably both.

I eventually ended up sitting huddled against a wall near a pub I knew would be open until the small hours, so I knew people were there but they didn't know I was.

It was comforting in a way, hearing distant voices, music, life. On the other hand, it somehow made me feel oddly excluded, not just the fact I would be kicked out if I dared go in and ask for a drink (one could tell I was so not eighteen, especially when I was wearing my torn jeans and worn out sweat shirt, my badly dyed hair scrunched up into a ponytail, not to mention the bad skin). Just sitting there on the outside of everything, knowing you didn't belong.

I knew Greg and Phoebe would have realized I was missing. I knew they'd be worried and that bloody Mrs. Harris` prejudiced thoughts about me had probably pretty much been confirmed.

I knew Cam would be wondering why I wasn't at school and would, at the same time, be guessing I'd done something stupid. Al would be keeping an eye out for me in the lunch break, as usual. And somewhere, in the very back of my mind, I knew I had to take some responsibility and do something sooner or later.

So I plucked up my courage and, after spending hours in a café nearby and the rest of the cash I had on me on coffee, I went to wait for Cam outside school.

She burst into immediate tears when she laid eyes on me. "I just thought you were off sick. But then Mr. Draper came up to me and asked whether I'd heard anything about you because your foster dad called in sick and said you hadn't come home last night and I thought you'd gotten yourself into real trouble."

I felt ashamed. But I also felt there had been nothing else I could have done than literally run away from everything for a moment.

"I'm sorry." I said and gingerly opened my arms, not sure whether she fancied a hug from me right now. But she willingly walked towards me and hugged me back.

"Where were you?" she asked as she released me with a final sniff, wiping her eyes.

I shrugged "Just outside, sorting things out."

"Outside? Are you effing bloody mad? You'll get pneumonia! Why didn't you come to mine if you were too scared to go home?" I could tell she was angry now. I shrugged once more. Why not indeed? Because I had difficulties trusting anyone, even my very best mate? Because I felt like I might start breaking stuff any minute? No idea.

Greg and Phoebe were notified that I was back.

Greg came into my classroom at one point shyly peering round the door.

I was excused and went outside to meet him. Apparently, the two of them had been devastated, as the first thing Greg did when

I stood before him was gather me into his arms and start weeping.

I felt terrible.

"What were you thinking, Lynni? Where *were* you?" he gulped when he'd managed to calm down.

"We were worried sick! Phoebe called in sick in case you came home. What happened?"

But how could I tell him what had happened?

"Nothing." He looked at me yet more questioningly.

"I'll tell you later?"

I could tell he still wasn't happy but let go of my shoulders and nodded sadly. "You know you can tell us anything, Lynni?" his blue eyes still glistened with tears of genuine concern. "We love you."

I gulped. "I love you too."

He nodded, gingerly, ruffled my hair and gestured for me to return to my classroom.

At lunchtime I had a very similar conversation with Al…

Lynne, 1999

Everything that occurred in the following hours…even weeks or months…was like watching an extremely long, tiring movie. Like I was sitting in the cinema, in a daze, only just able to follow the tough storyline while my bum went numb.

Cam went home with me, chatted away anxiously to make us both feel better. I was thankful, in a way. And it kept me from running away from everything yet again, to a future where I would sit in cafes and perpetually drink coffee until…something happened.
She held her hand out to me and I willingly took it as we approached the living room where, to my horror, not only Greg and Phoebe were waiting t the coffee table, but

also Mrs. Harris, who was smirking nastily into her syrupy tea, and Al.

I breathed, gulped and mumbled a quiet "I'm sorry."

Phoebe got up and embraced me as Greg had earlier. "What on earth happened, Love? We were all worried!"

"Come and sit down." Greg patted a chair between him and Phoebe and gestured to a steaming cup of tea and a plate of biscuits.

Cam gave my hand a final squeeze and I sat down, not daring to look in Al's direction. I could feel his gaze on me while I sipped my tea. Everybody was waitig for me to say something, apparently. I was feeling very uncomfortable. Phoebe put her hand on mine after she'd sat down next to me. "Come on, Love. Tell us what's wrong, we want to help you."

I thought about asking Phoebe to come into the kitchen with me. Perhaps it would be more bearable just telling her without the whole world sitting there, looking concerned. I felt sick.

"Lynne?" I heard Cam's voice. I she had a squirmy air about her, like she was suffering just as much as I was.

Or maybe Al? Shouldn't he be the first to know? Maybe he'd know what I should do?

Oh bloody well, who cared anyway.

I took a deep breath. "I'm pregnant." I daren't look up. I crammed a biscuit into my mouth and chewed noisily to fill the silence. The air was so thick one could cut through it.

"Well…" oh crap, Mrs. Harris would be the first to say something vile. "What a surprise." She drawled. "Phoebe, this is utterly inacceptable!"

"Oh, Mu – "

I could feel Phoebe's and Greg's protective hands on either side of my shoulders and heard Mrs. Harris spitting hateful comments in our direction, but was too busy swallowing and then fighting the approaching nausea. I heard Phoebe and Greg, everyone was getting louder. I was getting dizzy. I felt hands on mine, pulling me to my feet. I was in the living room, in the hallway…

Al's hands on either side of my face as he tried to get through to me.

Al's voice. "Lynne! Look at me."

Cam's voice. "She's falling, Alan. Catch her!"

Next thing I knew, I was lying on the sofa with Phoebe and Cam kneeling beside me.

I had a headache and didn't quite know what was going on.

Cam was holding my hand and Phoebe was gently stroking my forehead.

"Are you alright, Sweetheart?"

I nodded.

I sat up carefully and she handed me a drink, then I turned around – a little too abruptly, as I felt like I was going to go down face first into the potpourri on the coffee table - to make sure Mrs. Harris wasn't sitting there, ready to make her next inappropriate comment.

"It's fine, it's just us." Phoebe soothed me, noticing my unease. I relaxed a bit. "Where is everyone?"

"I got my Mum to go to bed a minute ago. She was…frazzled. And Greg and Alan have gone for a walk and talk."

I hoped Greg wasn't being too hard on Al, but I didn't think he would be.

"How long was I out cold?"

"Not even five minutes. You just had a bit of a fright…"

I just sat, looking down at the glass in my hands. I knew someone was going to start speaking about IT any minute. It was, after all, inevitable.

Cam was sitting next to me, silent for once. Phoebe made a little, insecure coughing sound and then said "Sweetheart, why…sorry if you're uncomfortable with this whole thing but we have to talk about it…why didn't you use protection?"

Wow, she was obviously more tolerant than I'd expected. Then again, Phoebe seemed to be one of these people who remembered what it was like to be young and stupid and impulsive.

"I...we..." we *had* taken preventive measures of sorts but I really, *really* didn't feel like going into the exact details with Phoebe. Or Cam, as a matter of fact.

"We did. But it appears to not have worked."

She nodded understandingly, empathetically, even. "We'll need to think about how we're going to go about this. But, Lynne, everything going to be ok."

I nodded, then briefly met her gaze. "Do you hate me?"

She cupped my face in her hands to hold my gaze. "Never." Then hugged me tight.

She took me the gynecologists the next morning and he confirmed that a) I was healthy and had a very nice uterus, b) yes, I was pregnant and c) eleven weeks.

After having a private, very awkward talk with him about what the fuck I should or could do, he told me the options that, as it was too late to abort, either find a way to cope with being a mum while finishing school etcetera (with the help of family and friends, for instance) or I could give him or her up for adoption and would basically not have to worry about the situation anymore after giving birth.

I didn't want to think about it, wanted to disconnect myself from my physical state until it was over and never have anything to do with it again.

Sadly, that's not how life worked.

Greg and Phoebe were supportive and, to my relief, never spoke about it more than absolutely necessary (Phoebe DID however, at some point, insist we I talk to the gynecologist about birth control and the like), as were both Alan and Cam.

Alan and I, as a matter of fact, decided shortly after all this happened that we were together. Not just because of the situation, because we were quite smitten with one another and it was working out very well.

School was hellish, having to cope with stares and annoying reactions and questions as my stomach started to grow, revealing what was going on inside me.

But the worst part was that I no longer felt comfortable going to the place I'd begun to see as home afterwards.

I went to Al's after school and spent many Friday nights at Cam's, dreading the fact that, at some point, I'd have to leave the Lawsons to their own, peaceful life and go back to Greg and Phoebe's.

It wasn't them, not at all. It was the discomfort Mrs. Harris caused each and every fecking day with her comments and looks and her mere presence.

It was clear that she wanted me out. She said this with the way she behaved towards me, but also stated this quite openly more than once while I was within hearing distance.

It was making me sick and I knew for a fact that Mrs. Harris wasn't going to be leaving any time soon.

It made me feel terrible and sad, especially because I'd thought I was finally getting to settle down a bit. No...It would be unfair to insist that Phoebe change something about the Mrs. Harris situation when she was her mother and I was just a girl they'd known for a relatively short time. But I couldn't do this to myself.

When I was just over seven months, Phoebe asked me whether I'd decided what I was going to do "after". I had. I couldn't have anything to do with this. I just didn't feel like I was connected to this thing inside me in any way. I simply didn't want any of this.

And so she helped me, or rather took over, looking for couples willing to adopt a newborn baby in about two months time.

I was an utter mess at that time. And so, Phoebe and Greg had the people over and talked to them over tea and biscuits and finally decided on a couple that were appropriate. That was enough for me. The baby would be fine. I would be fine. Mostly. After a while.

Al had, of course, asked once or twice whether I was really sure about all this and I sensed that he didn't entirely hate the idea of us being mum and dad. But he respected my decision and I loved him for that.

Cam also made several attempts to talk me into how nice it might be to have a little baby. I know she only meant well. But no. Me, a mum…it wouldn't work for either of us.

It all went very quickly. After my water burst (in the middle of maths…of course it was in the middle of maths), Greg took me to hospital immediately and then contacted Phoebe and Al, who came shortly after and they all waited.

It was painful - like, bloody fecking painful - but it was over and done with quick and without complications.

I held the baby for the first and last time, not able to cry, not able to smile. I felt a pang of something - Relief? Pain? Love? - inside me. Telling me not to let go, ever.

Once he was clean, Phoebe and Greg took turns holding him. Then Al, his face contorted with pain. Later on I hated myself for taking him away from Al. But still I felt that it would, in the end, be the right thing for everybody.

I shook hands with Quentin and Jessica Lennox and handed him over soon after and that was the last thing I'd ever have to do with any of it.

It didn't change the way Al and I felt about each other. Or Phoebe and Greg and I. It could have gone on the way it had for the past months but I knew what had to happen.

"Phoebe?" I said two weeks later when we were watching TV and Mrs. Harris was already in bed.

I'd hoped her verbal abuse might have stopped or at least reduced itself afterwards, but it hadn't. And still, Phoebe failed to protect me from it.

Phoebe and Greg both looked at me, eyebrows raised in anticipation. I rarely addressed someone with their name, so they realized I wasn't just about to ask for a raise on my allowance.

"I think I have to leave."

They looked at each other, lips slightly apart with fright, then back at me.

Greg then got up, patted me on the head fondly and left the room, sensing this might not quite be his place. Or perhaps to hide his shock, I didn't know.

"Leave?" Phoebe said finally after she'd switched off the TV. "How do you mean? Right now?"

But of course she knew what I meant. It wasn't just about going to Al's or to Cam's for the night anymore.

I shook my head, avoiding her gaze. "I love you. But I can't do it anymore."

Phoebe looked taken aback. "But-"

"Not you. Or Greg. Your Mum."

Her expression of pain turned into that of understanding. "I could...well...she's not a well woman but maybe if I talked to her again?"

I considered it but shook my head. She had. So had Greg. "It won't change."

Phoebe's eyes welled up as she came across the sofa and embraced me.

She didn't try to convince me otherwise, selfless as she was. She knew what I'd been through in many of the other homes during my whole childhood and knew it had to change.

We sat there, in silence, hugging each other and crying for a small infinity until we were able to speak.

Greg reacted in a similar manner, tears streaming from his gentle, blue eyes. But couldn't we find a way? This was an outrage what Georgina was doing to our Lynni! She'd have to go! But she needed the care more than I did, I said to keep the peace. And I was a big girl.

I was terrified that Greg and Phoebe, who were usually so happy and so in love, would have a fight about it. I'd never seen either of them so cross. I knew it wasn't because of me, but because of the situation. Though they'd have every right to blame me for everything…

But the first outburst subsided quickly and we were able to think.

We contacted my social worker and explained the situation, asking what options I had as I did not intend on going back into care.
I'd go to a half-way-home and do my exams, then find a job with Anita's help.
And then I'd take it from there, I supposed.

There was no sign of guilt or regret to be seen from Mrs. Harris when she heard the news. She simply huffed (triumphantly?) and muttered. "Ungrateful. Well, good riddance."
Old bitch.

I didn't own much so moving was easy. We decided we would stay in touch ("You're still our girl, Sweetheart, no matter what happens.") and that was that.

There wasn't much time left before my exams, which I was glad about. I couldn't face school anymore. It was as though I was fighting with all my strength to just keep going. Keep functioning. Until I was done and then finally got to break down.

Everything had suddenly caught up with me.

My childhood. My mother. My foster families. The bullies. The abuse.

I felt worthless. Guilty. Tired. Like I'd never be able to love or trust myself no matter how much love anyone sent my way. Couldn't love or trust anyone back.

I told both Phoebe and Greg and Cam and Al that I needed to be alone for a while.

Al respected this, as did Cam in a way. But neither of them ever failed to have an eye on me.

Round about that time I had my first cigarette and also my first drink with some of the other youths living there. I never took to any of them very much. I preferred my own company.

I did, on the other hand, take to nicotine and alcohol. Latter helped me block out the feelings and thoughts gnawing at me constantly.

It was good, in a way, that Cam and Al were still around even though I'd asked to be alone. They helped me through that horrible time until I was, at last, back on my feet, both literally and figuratively.

I never lost my love for photography and talked to Anita about whether I might have a future in a job involving photography.

With her help, I found a studio that was taking on trainees and, after applying, actually got the job.

I saw Cam and Al in between working and studying. I was, for once in my life, at peace.

Lynne, 2016

How could this be happening? There *had* to be a mistake. Things like this didn't happen! I was glad to come home to find Miles there. I would have gone bonkers with my own rotating thoughts and needed someone to slow them down.

I was back together with Al, in a way. But was still living with Miles as we were taking it really, really slowly. I still felt too vulnerable and it was all too delicate to go plunging back into a proper, full-blown relationship with living together and marrying and arguing about shopping lists and whatnot.

He looked up from his sandwich and looked mildly irritated. "Whassup with you?"

I collapsed onto the sofa next to him, not knowing where to start.

"You know Ben…"

"Yeah, 'course I know Ben." He said, visibly worried, gesturing for me to carry on.

"Something happen?"

"Kind of…"

I started from the beginning. No gory details, just the basic outline of the plot. I didn't look at Miles but could sense his expression changing with every sentence. After I'd finished, we sat in silence as I exhaled, and slowly stopped trembling.

"So Ben…he might be…" he concluded as he put one and one together.

I nodded. "He is."

"Oh my…" Miles exclaimed, rubbing his temples. "This is just pure madness! What are you going to do?"

"I don't know."

I had to talk to Ben. I knew I had to. And Al at some point. But how? All three of us

together? Or one after the other? But who first? And what if I was wrong?
But I couldn't be. That man had been Quentin Lennox. And those hazel eyes…They had Al written all over them. Of course I only came to realize that now that I knew.

The decision was taken from me mere minutes later when the doorbell rang and I opened the door to – what a surprise! – Ben.
"Hi…"
"Hi."
Miles got up, brushing the crumbs off his shirt, and scratched the back of his head awkwardly. "Should I go or…?"
I nodded, grateful for him being tactful, and he left the flat after doing one of those guy-handshakes with Ben.

Then Ben looked back at me. "What was that all about, then?"

I exhaled audibly, trying to calm my nerves. "Come on and sit down."

I got us both a drink and then sat down next to him.

I finished my story, once again leaving room for interpretation but I could tell by Ben's expression as I took a quick glance at his face that he got the idea. After a few seconds he started to giggle and slapped his thigh, like you do? But in a situation like this? Really? I smiled. Come to think of it…

"Bollocks!"

My smile faded. "What?"

"C'mon, Lynne. I mean it's funny and all but seriously?"

His own smile faded when he realized I was being sincere.

"What the…"

I nodded. "Yep."

"You're absolutely sure that Quentin's *that* Quentin?"

"Yep."

He blew up his cheeks and exhaled slowly while slumping back onto the couch, his expression blank.

I was surprised and slightly relieved as I'd expected him to storm off in the a similar manner as I had a few hours previously.

Once the news had sunk in we contacted Sandra, Ben's social worker, and when we met she confirmed that yes, I was Ben's biological mother.

This was real scary stuff. It explained so much on the one hand and on the other…boy was this a small world we lived in.

"So…what now?" I asked gingerly when we were back at my flat. Would this change everything? Would we let it? How did Ben now feel towards me? It was I, after all, who'd given him up when he was just a day old…bereaved him of a real mum and a real dad. Then again, until Jessie Lennox had gotten ill, her and Quentin had given Ben a home and a lovely childhood. Still…

Ben shrugged. "I don't know. It's pretty weird."

"Are you angry?"

He shrugged again, then looked at me and sighed. "What for? You were, like, my age when you had me. I don't think I could cope."

I moved across the couch an inch and rested my head on his bony shoulder. "Thanks."

We'd never have a regular Mum-Son-Relationship. It was too late for that. But that was ok, I supposed…Still, it would take quite some time to get my head around it…

"What about..you know. My Dad? My actual Dad?"

I straightened up, my heart giving a jolt. Of course! Al! Al was his Dad!! The bloke he was working for!!! How bloody weird was *that*!? I felt dizzy and nearly laughed out loud.

"Oh gosh, right…"

"What?"

"You know Alan…your boss at Little John's?"

"Yeah?"

"Well…yeah…" I scratched my head, feeling slightly uneasy. This was getting too much to digest for one evening. What must it be like for the poor kid?

He looked at me, wide eyes, his face unmoving. "You must be kidding me."

I shook my head and, in the next moment, burst into tears.

Perplexed as he was, Ben still managed to put his arms round me clumsily and let me sob onto his shoulder. A very awkward moment for both of us.

We sat there until I calmed down and dried my eyes and nose on my sleeve. "I'm sorry." I whispered, trying to stop bawling for good. "I'm sorry."

"It's ok." He patted my shoulder and looked at me. "Really, there's nothing to be sorry for."

I nodded and sniffed one last time. "Ok." And took a deep breath.

We looked at each other and I saw the corner of Ben's mouth twitching. Was he about to bawl his eyes out too? But to my outmost surprise, he let out an incredulous snigger.

"It's quite funny if you think about it."
I did. I thought about the whole situation, and couldn't help but smile too. It was.

I gave Alan a call the next day and asked if it would be ok to come by, I had something to tell him.
Sandra, Ben and I met and went to Little John's where we were seated and ordered drinks.
Sandra was a nice, middle-aged woman with a blonde bob and brown eyes. She was quiet, but I could imagine she was someone who would take no nonsense.
Al spotted us and smiled, looking mildly surprised when he saw Ben and Sandra.
"Hi." He shook Ben's hand, who smiled shyly while not taking his eyes off Al, and then held it out to Sandra. "Alan."

"Sandra. I'm Ben's social worker."

"Should I just take a seat or would you rather go outside?"

He must have sensed it wasn't something that involved me but Ben, Sandra being his social worker, and wasn't quite sure how to behave.

I shrugged. "Maybe we could just go out front for a minute?"

"Ok."

I wasn't sure how to feel about this whole situation. Of course we had to say something, but I couldn't help but worry a bit about his reaction. We'd just managed to get close to each other again, I hoped this wasn't too much all at once. Still, to just keep them away from each other or worse, have Ben working for Al every week while withholding the truth from Al would be cruel and selfish.

Once we were outside, I resisted the temptation to have a cigarette against my increasing nervousness and took a deep breath.

"You're in for a bit of a fright." I warned him and his brow furrowed.

"Alright? What's up?"

I could tell Sandra was nervous and Ben even more so, but it was only right they were both here.

"You know that thing that happened when we were young that we never really talked about again?" I still had problems naming it? This was ridiculous.

He nodded slowly and his eyes lit up in sudden comprehension. "Yeah?" he glanced at Ben, then back at me.

"Well." I took hold of Ben's sleeve and pulled him towards me. "Alan, may I introduce you to our son?"

Alan's expression was blank. "What…"

I nodded. There was nothing left to say.

"You? How?" he scratched the back of his head and paced back and forth for a minute.

"I think I need to sit down."

We led him back inside. Ben's smile had faded and a look of anxiety had crept into his eyes. He looked at me with a worried expression. I wanted to comfort him but all I could do was shrug.

Al gestured for us to come into the kitchen. It was quiet as there were only very few guests due to the time of day.

"Could someone?…"

Sandra took over, which I was very grateful for, and I let myself relax while putting my arm round a very nervous and mixed-up Ben.

She explained how, after Ben had been adopted by Quentin and Jessie, he'd led a normal life until Jessie had sadly passed away and he'd been moved on to different foster homes. And how I'd found him after he'd run away and we'd been pals, not knowing what was actually going on until I'd met Quentin and recognized him.

"Some may call it fate." Sandra concluded, shaking her head and smiling. "Some may call it a huge, massive coincidence. But, yes. This is your son." She gently shoved him towards Al.

Now the news had started to sink in, his expression had changed from shock and disbelief to something else. A tender look crept into his eyes. "Really?" he whispered. All three of us nodded.

A smile spread across Al's face and he opened his arms ever so slightly. Ben picked up on the gesture and walked into them and it was such a pure, genuine thing to watch as they gingerly held each other, Al now sobbing uncontrollably and muttering "My boy, our boy…" into Ben's hair. The two of them so alike in appearance and in nature.

Sandra nodded at me and made her own way out, sensing her job was, at least for the time being, done.

Al looked up and gestured for me to join in. I hesitated. "I'm sorry."

He smiled and nodded at the space they'd made for me to squeeze in. And I did.

I knew that I'd never be a real, proper Mum to Ben. That had been Jessie Lennox' role. But I could be a friend and Al could most certainly be a Dad. And maybe, just maybe we would manage to grow together as a family, of sorts.

When I sat on the settee that evening, half a roll in front of me, waiting for Miles to come home, there was something very different about the way I felt. It wasn't caused by one thing alone. It wasn't the relief of seeing that I had another job coming up for a major photo-shooting the following week. Or the perspective of everything, bit by bit, falling into place at last and making peace with my past and everyone involved.
No, I realized as I stubbed out my – at least for now - final cigarette.
I'd made peace with myself.
I'd started to forgive myself

Ben, 2016

Lynne was in London doing this big photo-shooting. She was thinking about moving in with Al, though they were still taking things slowly. How slowly and what exactly their relationship involved, I didn't really want to think about.
As for me, I would continue living with the two guys in our living community for how long it took to finish studying etc. I'd taken to both of them and I could still see Lynne and Al on a weekly basis.
I was still working for Al. It was a bit awkward at first, the whole thing, but we're relaxed around each other now.
I'd finally managed to ask the pretty girl with brown eyes, Susan, out. We'd gone to the cinema but I didn't quite know yet whether I'd be seeing more of her or not.

I'd even been to see Quentin. He was still drinking but I hoped I could help him a bit with that.

While Lynne was away, I was in charge of dropping in to get the mail in etc, as Miles had taken time off from Bigg's during the semester break to visit his dad in Newcastle.

Apparently, he'd lost his mum as well and had moved up north a couple of years ago in order to cope with it all and to recover.

I opened the letterbox, which wasn't very full. It contained an official looking letter addressed to Miles – probably a bill - and one for Lynne, her full name and address spelled out in what appeared to be a man's handwriting.

I had the instruction to read hers and to give her a call if it was something important, so I took them inside and eased the envelope open.

A card. An invitation? Yes an invitation. To Carl and Camilla's wedding.

Who were they?

Inside was the date, time and address of the whole event and that there would be food and drink and entertainment etc. and that they would be delighted to see "you" there.

Yours,

Carl and Millie

Of course, Millie was the woman, the editor Lynne had been working for all over Europe. They must be inviting employees as well as family and friends.

On the other half was a photograph showing the couple.

Something struck me as familiar about the woman. I was about to put it on the coffee table and water the plant (yes, there was

only one) before going to collect some chips for the three of us and then home to study. But then it hit me. Of course, that was the woman from one of Lynne's portraits I'd been sorting. The woman with the doe-eyes and cropped hair, looking over her shoulder. This was her. A few years older, perhaps. But definitely her.
Lynne'd never mentioned knowing this Millie already. Had she? Maybe they just really looked alike... Huh. Weird.

Cam, 2016

It was cold. I feared there might be an early snow. But I'd wanted a long fairy-princess dress, so I'd decided against marrying in the Summer I'd been a bit disappointed when Carl had told me he wasn't comfortable with a big wedding and why not just have our family and closest mates. Carl was rather quiet and steady, but he was also witty and clever and liked to surprise me. And so, he'd invited relatives and friends from all around and even many of my employees so that I could have the day I'd always wanted so badly.
This was absolutely fine.
The ceremony was over and done with. The days of sobbing into ice cream buckets was – hopefully – over and I was absolutely over

the moon. Carl was lovely. There he was, waving at me while munching a canapé. I'd have to do that glass clinking thing soon to get everyone to sit down for the meal. I hoped everyone would have room after all the shrimps and prosecco!

When everyone was seated, I smiled to myself as I scanned the crowd of people. There were my Mum and Dad next to my Auntie Bella and my Grandpa. And so many others. Clara and Annie, and Carl's mates from uni, Trevor and Lisa. And...she was further away but I knew that face, that hair, that girl. But how? Of course. All my employees. Models and designers and photographers. And she'd come.

My eyes welled up with tears. No one else saw, as they were still busy chattering away and un- and refolding papers with their speeches they wanted to recite. In this vast

amount of people of all ages and shapes
and sized, it was as though we were the
only two people in the world.
I gingerly raised my hand to wave hello.
And she waved back.